Beastly Savage

MK Richberger

Three-Eyed Cat Press LLC

Contents

Content Warnings

This book is not suitable for anyone under the age of 18.

RATING: M

WARNINGS: DEATH, BLOOD/GORE, talk about drugs, sex, knife play, blood play, kidnapping, suggested rape, murder, abuse.

One

Adam

ONCE UPON A TIME, I was a prince who threw elaborate parties with the elites of the surrounding kingdoms. I spared no expense, supplying my guests with the best food, drinks, drugs, and even beautiful women. No one left unhappy.

After one successful party, high out of my mind, I stumbled down the corridor to the master bedroom. Reaching the door, a woman's voice met my ears. I pushed open the door, angered that my personal space had been invaded.

"Alright, get the fuck out!" I roared, sneering at the man kneeling over a woman on my bed. His face was hidden by the drapery above my bed, but I could see he was well built and, if he had been standing, would be a little shorter than me.

The naked woman scrambled back, twisting onto her knees to climb down. The man grabbed her by her fiery red hair, jerking her head back so her throat was exposed.

"Adam, about time you arrived." The voice cut through my high, sobering me in an instant. Gaston Mal, the man behind the most notorious mafia, Cinder Crew. The name was cringey, and I'd been known to make fun of it, but with Gaston leering at me from my bed... It was still dumb, but I wasn't stupid enough to say that to his face.

The woman cried as he positioned himself behind her, sinking his fingers into her hips, and pulled her to him. "Great party, Adam," he said, thrusting into the woman. She cried out, her long, crimson hair hiding her face as she dropped her upper body. "I've been wanting to talk to you."

"It had to be while you fucked this poor girl?" I pressed my lips together, disgusted by what I was witnessing.

Flipping the woman over so she was on her back, Gaston smirked at me. "Did you want a turn?"

"Get out."

Pulling his pants up, Gaston rounded the bed toward me.

"Adam, is that any way to greet your golden opportunity?" He rolled his sleeve up onto his biceps.

"You have nothing I want, Gaston," I grumbled, watching the woman hurriedly collect her clothes from the floor. "I'm a prince. I have all the money and power I need. With a snap of my fingers, I can have my people take care of you."

The woman pushed her hair from her face as she neared me. She barely glanced at me through the mess of mascara running down her face as I moved out of her way.

Gaston grabbed her arm, and she screamed as he pulled her to him. "I heard you have quite the talent with knives and archery." He pulled a knife from his pocket and held it to the woman's neck. "I want you on my crew."

"I don't know what you heard, but I want nothing to do with—"

He dragged the blade of the knife across the girl's throat. Her green eyes widened in shock, and her scream abruptly stopped in a gurgle. "I wasn't asking," he said, shoving the girl into me.

I fumbled, sinking to the floor with her, trying to apply pressure to her neck as blood poured from the open wound. She mouthed something at me, her eyes glossing over as her body went limp.

Behind me, the door opened, and a woman gasped. "What's going on in here?"

"He stabbed the poor girl," Gaston said dramatically, louder than was necessary. His words ricocheted around in my skull, the look on his face making the hairs stand up on the back of my neck.

I gaped at him. "What did you do?" I whispered, my stomach twisting in sick realization as an older woman stepped beside him. Priscilla Trevaine, Cinder Crew's other founder.

"Seems you have two options," she said, nudging the woman's head with the toe of her high heel. "Prison or join us."

I looked down at my once white shirt, now crimson in blood, and scowled. "You could have just asked."

Two

Belle

The princess cried out, hiding her face as the monster stepped toward her. She could feel its breath upon the skin of her neck. From the shadows, a wolf lunged, tackling the creature to the ground, and roared in its face. The princess gasped, taking the opportunity to run back to the safety of the castle. As she neared the thick doors, she looked over her shoulder just in time to see the wolf transform into a man. Not just any man, but the—

"Belle..." I startled, looking up at Jack dusting a nearby shelf. "You know I love having you here, but it's about to start getting dark." The elder librarian twisted his body toward me, a friendly but worried smile lifting his lips under his gray mustache.

I lowered my eyes to the book in my hands. "Oh, but Jack, I was at my favorite part." I stood, holding the book out to him. "No matter how many times I read this, I still get shivers when the monster attacks."

He chuckled and waved me off. "You keep the book, Dear," he said, returning to his tidying up.

"Keep it? Are you sure?" I hugged the book to my chest.

Jack nodded, motioning for me to follow him to the front of the shop. "Yes, yes. I know how much you love that book. You keep it. But hurry on home now. It's not been as safe around here lately. I couldn't bear to see something happen to you." He held the door open for me, his face falling as the streetlights lit up. "Go on. I'll see you on Monday morning. I have a shipment coming in that you can help me put away."

On my way out, I hugged him. "Thank you, Jack, thank you! I'll see you bright and early Monday." I heard him chuckle as I hurried down the sidewalk.

Since I was a child, I visited the little library almost daily. As soon as I was old enough, I put in an application and have worked there ever since. I read whatever I could on my breaks and after work before heading home to make dinner for my father.

It was wonderful, but I had big dreams I was saving for. One day, I would visit the many places I had only read about...

Rounding the building to the town square, I slowed near the fountain and flipped a coin into it, silently making a wish. As soon as the coin hit the water, I continued on my way.

When I arrived home at our little cottage, Papa was sitting on the porch swing. He rocked slowly, a wide smile breaking free of his bushy white beard. "Belle, my dear! How was your day?" He stood, enveloping me in a hug and a kiss on the cheek before opening the front door.

"Oh, Papa, it was a wonderful day! Jack even gifted me my favorite book so I can read it whenever I want." I swept through the house to the kitchen, the smell of beef stew making my stomach growl.

Papa laughed merrily, placing silverware on the small wooden table while I dished out the stew. "I'm happy for you, Belle. Do you have any plans for this weekend?" he asked, taking a seat.

I shook my head, placed a bowl and piece of bread in front of him, and sat with mine. "I finally have a free weekend, and I'm going to catch up on some reading." I sighed, excited to do nothing but lose myself in my favorite book.

"Gaston stopped by."

A shudder worked through my body at the name. The man was a stubborn brute who thought he could have whatever he wanted. He had been stalking me for years, determined that I would change my mind and accept his proposal.

"Why?" I scrunched my face up.

He wrung his hands. "He wanted to see you. I told him you weren't interested." Nodding to himself, he dipped his bread in his stew and shoved it in his mouth.

Dread twisted in my chest. "And he was okay with that?" Stubborn wasn't a strong enough word to describe Gaston. The man was relentless. He was even part of the reason my last relationship failed. It turned out I was seeing one of his employees. He made it abundantly clear that if I continued to see the man, there would be harm done to him. So I left him...

A slow blush crept across Papa's cheeks and nose. "He wasn't thrilled, but he left." He wiped his mouth on his napkin and smiled at me. "One day, I hope you're able to follow your dreams and travel the world. I hope you find someone nice who shares that dream with you so you're not alone."

I grabbed his hand, giving it a little squeeze. "Thank you, Papa."

"You know, I think you'd be a wonderful teacher!" he declared, a joyous belly laugh bellowing from him. "You're an amazing woman, Belle. I'm not surprised Gaston wants you, but I do wish he would leave you alone. *You* don't deserve a man like that."

Papa's words resonated within me, warming my heart. He was right. Gaston was a curse. Unfortunately, he was my curse to deal with.

Three

Adam

COLD COFFEE WAS LEFT in the pot, and I was already in a mood. Working with only two hours of sleep after the last week of cleaning up several of Gaston's messes, I was a string's width away from just snapping. I dumped the shit out in the sink, rinsed the pot, cleaned everything out, and started a pot of extra caffeinated cherry-flavored dark roast.

Smelling the coffee, Louis came slinking in. "Good morning, Adam!" He half sang, grabbed himself a mug, and cozied up to me, waiting for the pot to finish filling. The short, round man looked up at me and grinned, revealing his large, crooked teeth.

"If you think you're going to take any of my coffee, you're a bigger fool than I thought," I said, reaching around him to the pot and grabbed it. "You didn't even bother cleaning up last night's coffee."

His face fell as he watched me drain the entire pot into my thermos. "You won't even let me have a cup?" He held his mug in front of him, a hopeful smile lifting his heavy, round face.

I glared at him, shaking the last drops out into my cup. "No." I returned the pot to the coffee maker and went to the fridge. "You have two hands and a heartbeat. Make it yourself."

Pursing his lips, he stared at the empty glass pot. His shoulders squared up, and he twisted around toward me. "Gaston has his eyes on that pretty little thing that works at the library. Didn't you used to have a thing with her?" He nonchalantly began cleaning out the coffee maker, tossing the coffee grounds out into the trash, and thumped the filter against the side.

"I've been with a lot of women. You'll have to be more specific." I poured creamer into my coffee, glancing at him from the side of my eyes.

He bit his bottom lip, the corners of his mouth curled, and his eyebrows shot up. "You know... The one that loves to wear blue sweatshirts and has that nice. Tight. Ass."

He cupped his hands and mimicked squeezing said ass. I had to restrain myself from slapping him upside the head. "The one who works at the library," he reiterated.

Belle, he was talking about Belle... She was my 'The-One-Who-Got-Away.' We dated for a few months, but things got complicated when she discovered I worked for the Cinder Crew.

Snorting, I put the lid on my thermos and shrugged. "Alright, so Gaston's interested in her. So what?" I turned and sat on the counter, taking a slow sip of the scalding liquid.

Louis bounced on his heels. "He asked her father for her hand, and when he said no, you know what Gaston did?" He squealed in excitement about what he was going to say next, his face growing red. "He offered to *buy* her! And the moron *still* said no! Can you believe that! A chance to get out of that shoddy mud hole and the *idiot* turned it down!"

"Good for him," I said, pushing off from the counter. "Some things aren't worth money," I said, done with the conversation and ready to get on with my day. Louis, giggling like a psycho, halted me mid-step. I peered over my shoulder at him with raised eyebrows.

He stopped his bouncing and grabbed the now full coffee pot. "That won't stop Gaston. He gets what he wants no matter what. By the way... he wants to see you," he said, filling half his mug with coffee, the other half with cream, and then poured a nauseating amount of sugar in it.

I turned away, closed my eyes, inhaled deeply through my nose, and walked from the room. I made it halfway to Gaston's quarters when I heard Louis's heavy footfalls behind me. A moment later, he began to hum. Loudly. Nothing in particular, just the same note over and over. "Hm. Hm. Hm. Hmmm." He followed me to Gaston's office, catching up with a laugh when I stopped to knock on the door.

"This is going to be so much fun!" He squealed, balling up his fists in front of himself excitedly before letting himself into the room with a skip. I took a long drink of my coffee, savoring the distracting burn, before following him.

Gaston was sitting on his throne in a grey designer suit that looked more expensive than my car. His lips twisted in a snarl, watching Louis tidy up the room. He looked like he was going to say something to the small man, then noticed me. "Beast," he said, perking up as he stood and approached me. "I heard you were successful! I already deposited your money and added a bonus to restock your arrows." He belted out a laugh, and I cringed. I'd never used arrows the entire time I 'worked' for the man. My weapon of choice was knives, sometimes a gun. But never arrows. Archery was something I kept for myself. It was the one thing he couldn't take from me.

Picking up and spilling out the contents of a coffee mug, Gaston set it down on its side and watched in amusement as Louis hurried over to clean up the mess. Twisting on his heel, Gaston smirked at me. "I hope you're not too tired. I have an important mission for you! You see... I am in search of a wife. Not one of those trained, dull-eyed sluts Priscilla has. A *real* woman. An elegant one who will make my meals and service my cock, while also not afraid to put me in my place."

The burning in my mouth was not enough to erase the mental image he placed in my head. "Wonderful," I muttered, looking around for a pen or something to stick in my eye.

Clasping me on the back, he led me to the desk in front of the window and pulled back the curtains. "That's where you come in, my man!" He leaned against the desk, pointing out the window at the small town below our castle window. "There. You see that woman sitting at the fountain? Brown hair, blue and white sweatshirt? Her. I *want* her."

Surrounded by children, Belle sat on the edge of the fountain, reading a book. I scratched my jaw and shrugged.

"That one? Why don't you talk to her then?" The suggestion alone made me nauseous. The thought of him even being *near* Belle made me want to slit his throat.

Louis bubbled in laughter. "Oh, he has! Haven't you, Gaston? He's asked for her hand more times than I can count!" He hesitated, staring at a lamp made to look like a human skull, and frowned at it.

"Louis!" Gaston shouted, the veins in his neck jutting out as he slammed his hand on the desk. The little man cringed, ducking his head into his arms at the sound. "Shut your fucking mouth!" Gaston roared, saliva flinging from his lips.

"Yes, sir!" Louis laughed, scurrying to the other side of the room.

Gritting his teeth, Gaston breathed in sharply through his nose and slowly turned back to me. He stared at me wildly for a half second, then smiled. "As I was saying..." He wiped the spit from his chin and composed himself.

Taking a drink of my coffee to stop myself from commenting about his ridiculous outburst, I nodded for him to continue.

"I asked Belle's father for her hand, but he turned me away. The old man doesn't know what's good for him, let alone

Belle. I called in a favor with a friend at the police station. While Belle is at work, Reece will be arrested for money laundering. When Belle gets home, I need you to collect her for me and bring her to my guest house." He flopped down on his throne with a satisfied sigh.

Through the window, I watched Belle stand and leave the fountain in the direction of the library, my shoulders tensing. "Shouldn't you be the one to get her? I'm your hitman. I don't kidnap."

"No, no. You see..." He leaned his elbows against his knees, a giddy smile washing across his face. "You *will* kidnap her, bring her back to my guesthouse where *I* will rescue her. After, I will save her father from prison, and they both will accept my marriage proposal." He went back to the window, frowning as he noticed she had left. "And if she doesn't, then I'm sure Priscilla would enjoy having her," he said darkly, the amusement dissolving from his face.

I pressed my lips together and nodded. "Genius," I mumbled. "And if I decline?"

Louis froze, dusting a picture frame, his arm mid-wipe as his eyes darted over to Gaston to see his reaction to my question. Even from across the room, I could see the man's Adam's apple bob and his breathing stop.

Gaston's eyebrows shot up, and he snapped his head in my

direction. His face worked through several expressions as though he hadn't even considered the idea of me turning down the job. "Decline...?" he drawled out, tapping his fingers along his chin.

A nervous chuckle escaped Louis's mouth. "What a silly question." He giggled, going back to cleaning, his hands visibly shaking now.

"Why would you turn this offer down, Adam?" Gaston tilted his head, the hamster in his brain really working the wheel. "I thought you'd enjoy this opportunity. Something... *different* to entertain yourself with. But if you don't *want* to, of course, you can say no." He went to his desk and pulled open a drawer, taking a thumb drive from it. "Have you noticed the news has been quite slow lately? They could use something new and exciting. I wonder how much they'd pay for a story about the prince murdering a young woman and going on a killing spree. Can you imagine? Not only a serial killer in this village but the *prince*!" He paused for a moment, his eyebrows narrowing. "Heard he even killed his parents before the police caught him."

Ice water rushed through my blood, and my mouth went dry. After the night Gaston 'recruited' me, I cut ties with my family once I realized how deep the Cinder Crew went. Shoving my hands in my pockets, I locked eyes with him.

"You want me to grab her tonight, then?"

"Tomorrow. Don't need you to fuck it up being hasty now. Don't give her any food for the first night." He dropped the thumb drive back into the drawer and slammed it shut.

I inched my way to the door. "Got it. How long will she be at the guest house before you... save her?"

He looked over his shoulder at me. "Two weeks. Be rough with her, Adam. Hire some guys if you have to. I want her broken and desperate for *me*."

Four

Belle

After breakfast, Papa was already downstairs in his workshop, working on his latest invention—some kind of kitchen appliance that not only cooked but also juiced things. It was one of his projects he liked to work on in between tinkering with clients' requests.

Usually, the sounds of him working were soothing and would fade into the background as I read. But today, I couldn't seem to focus. I collected my book and a small lunch, opting to pay Jack a visit and spend my afternoon in the quiet of his library.

I checked for any stains on my light blue shirt, smiled at myself, and went to the basement. Opening the door amplified the noises. "I'm going to the library!" I shouted over the clanging of metal. I'll see you tonight. Love you!"

The sounds abruptly stopped. "Leaving?" Papa appeared at the bottom of the stairs. "Was I being too noisy for you?" He ran a soot-covered hand through his beard, giving it a patchy grey look.

I shook my head. "It's okay. It sounds like you are enjoying yourself down there."

He laughed. "Is that how it sounds up there?"

Smiling, I shrugged and pointed to the kitchen. "I made you lunch and put it in the refrigerator. Try to remember to eat."

Grabbing a hold of his round stomach, he laughed again. "I could stand to miss a meal, my dear. You spoil me. I don't know what I'd do without you. Go, enjoy yourself. Love you!"

"Love you too, Papa," I said, closing the door to the basement. After checking to make sure I had everything I needed, I headed outside into the warm sun. It was a beautiful day, perfect for reading at the fountain before going to the library.

I made my way through town, greeting everyone who passed me by. The baker was in a heated argument with his wife, but both paused long enough to smile and wave to me as I walked past. I giggled to myself as they went back to their argument about his drinking.

A group of children raced past me to the fountain, jumping and playing on the edge. One even jumped into it, splashing the others. They all squealed in laughter before running off again. As soon as they left, I noticed a man standing near the fixture. I slowed, my heart lodging itself in my throat, worried for a moment that it was Gaston. With no one around, it'd be hard to avoid him—

It's not, it's Adam... The tension eased a fraction from between my shoulders, but my heart continued to pound against my ribs, yearning to be closer to him. *What's he doing here?*

His dark hair was freshly cut in a short fade, tussled as though he'd been running his fingers through it while waiting for me. Playing with his hair was a nervous habit of his that I found endearing. When he asked me out, his hair was a mess. My heart sank at the memory, and I wished with my all in that moment that fairytales were real and we could go back to that time...

Coming back to reality, I took him in. He was dressed in dark slacks and a matching vest, with a white shirt underneath, the sleeves rolled up on his biceps. A black shadow wolf wrapped around his left arm, disappearing under the sleeve. The whole ensemble was casual-looking with black and white high-top shoes. His honey-brown eyes caught the sunlight just right so I could see the flecks of green in them. "Hey."

"I have nothing to say to you," I said curtly, taking a seat on the edge of the fountain and folding my legs. I picked a thread loose from the inside of my jeans' leg and glanced up at him. Our relationship had been a flash in the pan. We met the previous summer while I was grocery shopping. He invited me to dinner, and it was immediate chemistry. The kind I've only ever heard about in my fantasy books. Even though we moved quite quickly with our relationship, he was a very private person. I didn't know what his occupation was for a few months. The most he'd tell me was that he was a businessman and had very important clients.

Unfortunately, after a few months of dating, I discovered that his boss was Gaston. The brute had been after me since he moved into our quaint little town. Worried about how he'd react to me dating his employee, I ended things. Not exactly in the nicest way, either... Gaston was an unstable stick of dynamite. Anything could set him off, and I didn't want it to be Adam... So I made up a fight and broke up with him.

Adam sighed, his head tilting back as though asking the heavens for a favor. I lifted an eyebrow, watching him, letting him have space to gather his thoughts. Rubbing the back of his neck, he lowered his eyes to mine and took a deep breath. "Then maybe you can just listen to me?" He scratched at the stubble on his chin.

Turning my attention to the children running toward the bakery, I nodded once. "I'm listening," I said, placing my book in my lap.

"I wanted to warn you... Gaston has plans to—" The group of children raced into the town square screaming, the baker red-faced and hot on their heels.

"You monsters!" he hollered, shaking his fist. "I know who your parents are!"

The group scattered, running down different streets and disappearing. The baker scoffed, muttering angrily to himself as he retreated back to his bakery.

I winced. "Sorry... You were saying?" I turned to Adam, finding him gone.

Five

Adam

THE AIR WAS THICK with cigar smoke, whisky, and tension. The radio droned on softly, some rock station Chris turned on before we lit up and poured drinks. We were exchanging war stories for entertainment, something to take our minds off the bullshit of being part of the Cinder Crew.

"Man, you should've seen it," I laughed, downing another shot of expensive scotch. "This bitch was begging for it. She couldn't get enough of me." I watched for Chris' reaction. Women loved the bad boy reputation the mafia brought. They flocked to us, playing hard to get. The moment they received any attention, their panties fell to the floor. Which was great trying to deal with a breakup.

A warm body to fuck away the pain with...

Chris sat across from me, leaning back in his leather chair with a smirk. "Sounds like your kind of night," he replied, his eyes glazing over as he stared at nothing. The smirk softened, slowly falling into a deep scowl.

"Hey, snap out of it," I barked, trying to yank him out of whatever thought was haunting him. "We're talking about fucking here, not your goddamn soul-searching."

"Sorry," he muttered. His eyes drifted to the brand on his forearm. The Cinder Crew logo. That cunt of a woman, Priscilla, gave it to him after he stepped out of line. The memory of the smell of his skin burning overcame the smell of cigars. I wanted to gag.

"Christ, Chris," I said, pushing the thought away. "You need to let that shit go. It happened years ago. You're still alive, ain't ya?" I slammed another shot to rid myself of the taste of bile.

"Alive, sure." He took a swig of his drink. The soulless look in his eyes made the hairs stand on the back of my neck. "But sometimes I wonder if there's any part of me left that isn't tainted by this fucked-up life."

Belle's face flickered in my memory. I scoffed, shaking my head. "You're just as twisted as the rest of us, man. That's why you're still here. You've got a taste for the darkness, same as me." The words tasted bitter. I washed them away with another drink.

"Maybe." Chris grinned, the action not meeting his eyes.

"Enough of this shit," I declared, slamming my glass onto the table. "We've got bitches to fuck and money to make. Let's get back to the good stuff."

For now, I had no choice but to play the role I'd been given – the ruthless mafia enforcer with a heart as black as coal.

"Alright," he agreed, clapping me on the shoulder. "Let's go show these whores what they're missing."

As we walked from the room, my thoughts turned to Belle. The girl who seemed to embody everything that I wasn't – light, warmth, goodness. And yet, it was my job to drag her down into the darkness with me. I couldn't help but wonder if there was any chance at all that she might be able to pull me back into the light instead.

I went home alone that night. I tossed my clothes on the floor and stood in the shower, washing the scent of cigars from my hair and skin. My mind raced about my orders and Gaston's determination to claim Belle as his own. Nausea sloshed around in my gut at the thought.

Gaston treated women worse than I'd seen him treat the dogs on the compound. They trailed behind him, wide-eyed and fearful, bruises on their faces. He didn't even try to hide the fact he was rough with them. He had them wherever he wanted, whenever he wanted.

I once knocked on his office, and he called me in as he was in the middle of ramming a woman against his desk. He grinned at me, her head yanked back by the hair and a knife pressed against her throat. He didn't even slow his pace as he spoke to me, barking out orders. Before I left, he ran the blade down the side of her neck and dragged his tongue up it, drinking the blood spilling out.

He didn't deserve someone as pure as Belle... I sure as hell didn't either. I was a monster. I'd done some awful things in my life, but the parties in my youth were the tamest part. I would give it all up, donate every single cent and thing I owned to charity if it meant gaining even an ounce of Belle's trust again.

Grumbling to myself, I shut the water off and stepped out, grabbing the towel hanging on the back of the bathroom door. Kidnapping Belle would be easy. Facing her was going to be the difficult part. I dried my hair and tossed the towel in the dirty clothes pile. Turning to my closet, the wolf skull mask hanging on the wall caught my eye.

"Fuckin' Gustov," Chris spat as he paced the warehouse, his boots echoing on the cold concrete floor. His shirt, soaked with sweat, stuck to his body as he clenched his fists, cracking his knuckles.

Lighting a cigarette, I popped it in my mouth and took a drag. Leaning back in my chair, I released my breath. "Relax, man," I said, holding the cigarette loosely between the corner of my lips, "It's not like you got a choice in this shit."

"Doesn't fuckin' mean I have to like it." Chris slammed his hand against a stack of crates, making them shake. "Gotta make this clean, fast. No mistakes."

I eyed the bleeding cut on his hand. "Got your back, Chris," I murmured, blowing out a puff of smoke. "Just say the word." It was best to say as little as possible when he was in a mood like this. I propped my feet up on a crate as he continued to pace.

"Don't need your help for this. Don't you have your own target?" He sighed, running a hand through his messy hair. "I'll need the van – black, no windows. Ropes, blindfolds, gag... the usual shit."

I held back the grimace. This wasn't the usual job. 9/10 it was: seek out the target, usually a male, and snuff him. But this... this was personal. There was something about this girl Chris held dear... and Priscilla knew it. I stubbed out my cigarette, crushing the butt under my boot. "What about the girl?"

"Already scoped her out," he growled, a lilt of guilt hanging in his voice. "Know her routine like the fuckin' alphabet."

"Damn, man." I chuckled at the confirmation of my thoughts. "Didn't know you were that into her."

"Shut the fuck up!" Chris glared at me, his jaw tensing. The expression wavered, a faraway look taking over as his eyes glazed over briefly.

"Whatever you say, man." I held up my hands in mock surrender, smirking as I sauntered away. "Preparations'll be ready by tonight."

"Great. You better go. Fucker probably has some chores or some shit for you to do." Chris shouted after me. I rolled my eyes. He was so caught up in his assignment that he already forgot I had told him about my assignment. Glancing over my shoulder, I shut my mouth, noticing Priscilla approaching Chris.

Six

Belle

I LEFT THE LIBRARY a little later than usual. Jack practically shoved me out the door, as usual. As I walked down the road to my cottage, unease raked its fingers up my back. The feeling of being watched followed me to the driveway. Every light seemed to be on in the house, making the strange feeling in my stomach grow. I ran to the porch, my heart leaping in my throat as I found the door ajar.

"Papa?" I called out, shutting the door behind me and locked it. "Papa, are you home?" Discarding my book on the coffee table, I went to the basement door and pulled it open. "Papa?" I yelled down the stairs.

"He's not home." A deep voice rasped behind me, sending

electricity up my spine.

I whirled around, slamming the door shut, and leaned against it. A large man stood on the other side of the room in a mask shaped like the skull of an animal with large sharp teeth, a black hoodie pulled over his head. I recognized the mask, but the sudden appearance of someone in my home jarred me, and I couldn't remember for the life of me where I'd seen it before. My heart slammed against my rib cage as he moved to the coffee table, picked up my book, and flipped through it.

"Who are you?" I whispered, my mouth going dry. "Where's my father?"

He looked up from the book. "The police took him." His tone was almost apologetic.

Taken off guard, I stepped away from the basement. He moved with me, and I stumbled back to the basement door, clinging to the doorknob like a life preserver. "Why?" Despite standing in place, I felt out of breath.

The man looked away from me to the front window. "Arrested for laundering money and fraud."

I tried to swallow the lump forming in my throat. Despite confidently standing in the middle of my living room, the man almost appeared to be distracted.

"Who are you?" I asked again, looking from him to the front door. *If I ran, I could make it and open it before he—*

"You locked it."

Startling, I snapped my attention back to him and tried to make myself look bigger and braver. I straightened up and squared my shoulders. "I knew that," I muttered, lifting my chin. Through the mask, I could see his mouth lift in a smirk, and a low, soft chuckle rumbled from him.

Holding my book out to me, he said, in a gentle but firm tone, "It's going to be a long ride."

Looking from him to my book, I shook my head, reaching for the doorknob behind me. "I'm not going with you," I said.

"You don't have any choice." His head tipped back in amusement. "Be a good girl and—"

I pulled open the basement door and nearly fell down the stairs, throwing myself through the door frame. The man made a deep guttural sound, cut off as I slammed the door shut, throwing the lock in place. He slammed his hand against it, the sound reverberating around me as I hurried to the bottom of the stairs and rushed for the window.

Shoving parts and pieces to the side of the desk, I climbed up and unlocked the window. Using my weight to unstick and shove it open, I crawled through the opening and into the soft grass, damp with the evening humidity. Once I had my legs out, I hoisted myself to my feet and ran—

Straight into the masked man's chest. His arms wrapped around me, holding me tightly to him. "Nowhere to run, little rabbit." He rumbled in my ear. I inhaled his scent, tobacco, and an earthy cologne. Again, there was a sense of familiarity for him. My brain clung to the recognition, unable to place where or who.

I tried to scream, but something pressed over my mouth, and everything went dark.

Adam

THE CELL WAS ALREADY occupied when I arrived with Belle. Chris had dumped off his target. The little thing stared at me through a mess of blonde hair as I shoved Belle inside. She woke up on the trip and gave me an earful the whole way. In the months we were together, I'd never heard her talk so foully as she kicked and screamed at the back of my seat. I had half a mind to lock her in the upstairs bedrooms instead but had a feeling Gaston would make a 'surprise' visit to make sure I'd done my job.

"Don't fuckin' move," I growled at Belle, pushing her against the stone wall. "Stay."

Jerking her arm free, she snarled at me, "Monster!"

"You have no clue, little rabbit," I said, matching energy. We locked eyes, and she seethed, practically panting in rage. "Just... stay here or—"

"Or what?" She challenged.

I wrapped my fingers around her throat, applying pressure, and whispered in her ear, "You'll find out how a rabbit actually feels when a wolf catches her."

When she didn't move, I released her and stepped away. Glancing at the disheveled woman watching us from the other side, I backed out of the room and shut the door, throwing the lock in place. With a heavy sigh, I removed the mask and carried it with me up the stairs.

As I had guessed, Gaston was waiting for me in the living room. He looked himself over in the mirror over the fireplace, flexing his biceps. Noticing me in the reflection, he turned, took the cigar hanging from his mouth, and grinned, revealing a row of near-perfectly straight teeth. "Beast, my man! How was your mission?" He approached me, slapping a hand on my back as he ushered me into the room. "Scotch? Whisky?"

"She's in cells like you requested. No." I waved him off, patting my pockets for my pack of cigarettes.

Gaston poured himself a shot glass and threw it back. "Perfect! I knew you were the one for the job. You probably noticed she has a little friend down there as well." He went back to flexing in the mirror.

"Sure." I shrugged, propping a cigarette between my lips while I searched for my lighter. "Little blonde mouse."

Lifting his arms over his head, Gaston chuckled. "Priscilla project. High-profile client"—he looked at me in the reflection and lowered his arms in front of his chest— "Gustav. Remember him? Man looks like a rat that's crawled from the sewers. Not sure how someone with so much money can look like *that*." He scrunched his face in disgust, looking for a moment like he might actually vomit.

Recovering, he interlaced his fingers and twisted his arms in front of himself. "He's got special plans for this one. Priscilla made him promise to keep her alive for at least a week to give her time for rounding up another." He took a step back, tipping his head back to look at the dark brown leather tapestry of large flowers above the mirror.

Bile rose in my throat. *No wonder Chris was acting like a caged animal the other night...* I lit my cigarette and took a casual drag, blowing the smoke at the ceiling. "Neat."

Letting his shoulders drop, Gaston faced me with a look that made the hairs on my neck stand. "Remember our agreement, Beast," he said lowly, his voice like venom in my veins. "You screw this up, Priscilla will ruin your life. Sitting in a prison cell rotting your life away would be a dream compared to what Fenrir would do to you if he found out you harmed Akari."

Furrowing my eyebrows, I glared at him. "What the fuck are you going on about? I haven't touched Akari."

A slow grin washed across his face. "Do you think it's a coincidence that you and Chris were chosen for these jobs? We know your sick fantasies. This is a reminder to keep you in line. Cinder Crew owns you... *We* own you, Beast. Get your rocks off one last time to your precious Belle. Do your job, Akari stays safe, and Fenrir won't claw your balls off."

My head swam with rage. *These fuckers and their fucking games...*

Gaston clicked his tongue. "Don't touch her tonight. There are no windows down there. She won't have any concept of time. Use that to your advantage. I want her putty in my hands when I return. Starve her, rape her, humiliate her, I don't care. Just break her." He blinked, glancing at himself in the mirror again, and smiled. "I'll be on a business trip for the next two weeks. You're free to stay here while you work." He walked past me and patted my shoulder, then motioned to a blinking light in the corner of the room. "Have fun."

I stared at the light, listening to the front door open and

shut. Tearing my eyes away from the camera, I watched him through the window, walk to the garage, and leave in an expensive sports car. I went to take a drag of my cigarette, finding it was nothing but the filter left.

"Fuckin' Gaston," I muttered, snubbing the butt in an ashtray on the table.

Seven

Belle

"Who the hell are you?" demanded a ragged, soft voice.

I faced the woman, her blue eyes wide with terror. "My name's Belle," I whispered, trembling from the adrenaline that had been coursing through my blood. As it slipped away, fear took its place, gripping at my insides. I glanced around the dark room, a single dying light bulb giving us almost no light. "They grabbed me and now I'm here... Just like that. One second, I'm free. The next, I'm in this hellhole."

"Stay away from me," the woman warned, backing up until her back pressed against the wall. Her eyes wandered over me slowly as though searching for something. The way she held herself, the expression on her face... *She's just like me.*

"Look, I don't want any trouble," I pleaded, wringing my hands, trying not to cry. "I'm scared shitless, just like you."

She sucked in a shuddering breath. "Scared doesn't even begin to cut it." She hesitated a beat, then added, "I'm Ella."

The tension eased in my shoulders. A break. Someone to lean on to get through this... "Got any idea why we're here?" I inched closer to her, the coldness of the room beginning to sink in. Jeans and a thin shirt provided very little protection in the low temperature.

"Fuck if I know." Ella sighed, the hardened expression on her face softening a fraction.

My heart sank, and the room suddenly felt a hundred times smaller. "God, what do they want from us?" I murmured, sinking onto the floor, and hugged my knees to my chest. "First, my papa is arrested, and then I'm thrown in here... what is going on?"

Ella shifted, tucking her blonde hair out of her face. For the first time, I could see her clearly. She was beautiful. The realization was like a knife to the chest. I'd read about women being kidnapped and sold in some of the books at the library. *Could this be one of those things...?*

"Survival, that's all we should focus on," Ella said, her eyes flickering to the cell door.

I nodded, swallowing hard. "Right... survival." If those books were right, then I was going to have to fight with everything I had to make it out alive.

We sat in silence for a long time. Letting the gravity of our situation wash over us and sink in. Footsteps outside the door sent an electric jolt up my spine. The door creaked open, and a brighter light flooded in briefly before the door slammed shut again, plunging us back into the darkness so thick it felt hard to breathe. The man fixed the bulb in the middle of the dungeon before turning towards us. He stood outside the light, mouth concealed with a black bandana, muscles taught, and tattoos littered across his arms and neck.

It wasn't the man who kidnapped me. His very presence made me feel nauseous. I glanced at Ella, her eyes locked on the man before us, her lower lip trembling. My heart slammed against my rib cage at her reaction.

"Please," she choked out, "you gotta let me go."

Her words didn't faze him at all. He just stood there, his tousled dark hair casting shadows over his eyes, giving him a demonic appearance.

"Listen to me," Ella begged, inching back as he opened the cell door. "I'm not who you want. I—I'm nobody."

He laughed, a low rumble echoing in the darkness of the room. He stepped forward, his eyes smoldering as he stared Ella down. "Nobody, huh?" He moved towards her. "When your father was appointed a Duke, you stopped being a nobody and became a somebody."

My eyes widened at this revelation. *A Duke... This wasn't just any woman... this was Ella Trevaine. Fuck, if I was being held hostage with her...*

"Dammit, Chris." Ella held her hands out toward him, reaching for something to hold onto. "I'm just a girl trying to live her life. I have dreams—"

"Everyone's got fucking dreams, princess." He leaned into her face, his voice lowering, "Yours just turned into a goddamn nightmare."

Gasping, Ella collapsed in a heap on the ground. I grabbed her hand as Chris retreated from the room, the metal door clanging loudly, leaving us alone once again.

"Hey," I whispered, "we'll get through this."

Ella's eyes shined with unshed tears in the dull yellow light. "How can you be so sure?'

"Because we have to." I squeezed her hand. "If we don't... I don't want to think about it."

She nodded, her throat bobbing as she blinked and turned to me. "What were your dreams, Bella?"

"Helping people," I whispered, thinking about the hours I had spent reading to the children at the fountain. I had dreams of traveling the world, but when it came down to it... Papa was right; I would love to be a teacher. "Making a difference... What about you?"

"Understanding minds," she said, suddenly laughing. There was no humor in the sound, only sad realization. She shook her head, sniffling. "I wanted to be a psychologist. To bring light to the darkest corners."

"You still can," I insisted, not wanting her to lose hope. It was such a lovely dream... "This isn't the end, Ella. We're more than what they think we are."

"More than pretty dolls in a fucked-up collection," she murmured. The statement shook me, but I couldn't let her see. I had to be strong for her.

"Exactly." I giggled to hide the fear in my voice. And when we're out, we'll chase those dreams down and make them beg for mercy." That's how the strong characters talked in my favorite books. They weren't concerned about what faced them, only their chosen outcome. My chosen outcome was revenge. No longer would I be poor, weak little Belle.

"Mercy," Ella echoed, her eyes ticking to mine as her lips lifted in a small smile. "Yeah. Mercy."

Our whispers wove together, a silent pact that bound us. In the pitch-black void, Ella and I clung to the one thing that couldn't be taken from us—not by force or fear.

Hope.

Eight

Adam

I BARELY SLEPT, THINKING about Belle alone in the dungeon. My mind raced with questions, plans, and scenarios—one hundred different ways I could murder Gaston. By eleven the next morning, I was surviving off the strongest coffee I could brew, watching Chris pace, spitting out curses every other breath.

"Get it together, man. There's not enough coffee in the world to deal with this today." I set my mug on the counter not missing the glare he shot at me. If looks could kill... I'd be dead one hundred times over.

"Fuck you," he snarled, raking his hands through his hair.

I rolled my eyes. "Spare me the attitude. We both know it's

not me you're pissed at." I grabbed the pot of coffee and filled my cup.

Chris twitched, nodded, and turned his attention to something across the room. "This can't be all there is," he muttered, stalking out of the kitchen. I watched him disappear in the direction of the camera room and sighed.

Drinking half my coffee, I abandoned the remains in the sink and made my way back to my room for my mask. It was close enough to noon to get things started with Belle. My chest tightened at the thought of harming her. But if it wasn't me, then Gaston would have someone else do it. And they for sure wouldn't hold back. I grit my teeth. No one else would be touching her if I had a say in it.

Taking the mask from my backpack, I headed down to the cells and slipped it on before opening the door. The two women looked up at me just like the cliché of deer caught in headlights. They huddled together, arms entangled as though it would anchor them to the spot.

I marched in, grabbing Belle by the wrist tight enough that her delicate skin would bruise, and yanked her from the floor. "Let's go," I said.

"I'll do anything. Just let us go," Belle begged, her body twisted away toward the girl on the ground. "Both of us. Please..." She stumbled into me as I pulled her across the room.

"You think this is some kind of game?" I growled, shoving her outside the cell, and slammed the door shut behind us. "You have nothing to bargain with, little rabbit."

She gasped, straining against me as I dragged her down the hallway. "I do not want to go with *you!* You're nothing but a monster!"

"Monster?" I grabbed her by the shoulders, slamming her against the wall. "You have no idea, darlin'." My stomach twisted with guilt. *It's me... Please... Realize it's me...*

Her eyes widened, and for a moment, I thought I saw a flicker of recognition in them. "Do... I know you?" she whispered, her head tilting in a vain attempt to see beneath the mask.

Yes... A memory from the fight that broke us up came slamming into me. I sorted through it, grasping onto something that would clue her in that it was me. I spun her to face the wall and leaned close to her ear. "I'm the monster *hired* to break you."

Belle's body tensed beneath my hands. She twisted her head to the side. "Who hired you?" she demanded, her face screwing up in anger. "Did Gaston hire you?"

I couldn't stop the grin from spilling across my face. I

knew she was smart. *Fuck Gaston and his plans.* "Can't say," I whispered, folding her arm behind her back. She whimpered as I applied pressure before yanking her away from the wall. "Let's go."

This time, she didn't resist me as I led her down the hall to the room where the Cinder Crew kept their 'toys.' It disgusted me, and I wouldn't be using any of them. I just needed the room to scare her. I opened the door, and her body stiffened at the sight of the various sex toys and contraptions throughout the room. I quickly pulled her out and slammed the door shut, bile rising in my throat at having even contemplated using the room.

"What... what was that?" she whispered, leaning into me.

"Training room," I responded, taking her into the empty room across the hall. It was in the process of being remodeled after Chris finished off one of his victims in the room. It wasn't his best idea, but Gaston had more than enough money to make the evidence disappear.

I released Belle, allowing her to move freely. She stopped at the window and turned to me. "Why are you doing this?"

"Did your friend tell you anything in there?" I asked, scratching my jaw beneath the mask.

She shook her head. "No... But... Are you going to sell us?"

Her eyes brimmed with tears, and she quickly looked away, swiping her hand across her face. "Is that it? And you're here to..."

I crossed the room to her and grabbed her by the chin. "You're not being sold," I told her firmly, my voice dropping slightly in empathy. "But you have to listen and follow my directions, or something worse than your worst nightmares will happen to you."

Jerking her face from my hand, she scowled. "What could be worse than *this*?"

"You're smart, little rabbit. I'm sure that pretty brain of yours could think of something. Or... someone." During the time we were together, I saw Gaston go after her once. The encounter was over before I made it to her. She had told him off and stormed away, meeting me with a relieved smile, and dragged me with her.

I grabbed her upper arm and pressed my body against hers. She tried to lean away from the mask, her eyes briefly shutting. "I don't want to hurt you," I said gently, brushing the side of her face with my finger.

"What do you want me to do?" she asked, bracing herself against me, her hand pressed against my chest. Once she looked at me again, I rolled my eyes exaggeratedly to the corner of the room where a camera was mounted. Her eyes flickered to it and back to me.

Releasing her, I motioned to her tight jeans. "Take your clothes off," I ordered.

Slowly, she revealed her curves, her nipples hardening as she exposed them. She held her clothes tightly to her body, goosebumps spreading across her arms. A deep red blush swept across her cheeks as she chanced a glance up at me. "Okay," she whispered.

"Drop them."

Hesitantly, she let the clothes fall to the floor and crossed her hands over her pubic area. I grabbed her wrists. "Let me see you," I said, dragging my fingers down her stomach. Her breathing hitched as I parted her. "Relax," I murmured, sliding my index finger and then middle inside her. She gripped my bicep, her body leaning into mine as I stroked her. "I'm not gonna hurt you... but I can't hold back either, do you understand?"

She nodded, and I pulled my fingers free, grabbing my hunting knife from my waistband. I unsheathed it and showed her the blade. Her eyes widened, shimmering in the dim light. "Are you going to kill me?"

"No. But I'm going to cut you and use your blood as lube." I growled, slicing the blade across her upper arm before she could react. She flinched, crying out as blood spilled, dripping to the floor. Her hand flew over the wound.

"What the hell!" she shouted, trying to back away from me.

I held her firm. "Do as I say, and this will be over faster," I snarled, sheathing the knife. "Lay on the floor."

Glaring at me, she lowered herself onto the carpeted floor. I knelt between her knees, pressing the handle of the knife between her legs. "I want you to come for me," I growled huskily, shoving the handle inside her pussy, making her gasp. While I thrust the knife inside her, I gripped her breast with my other hand, massaging the soft flesh and playing with her nipple. She moaned, her hips bucking into the hilt.

I moved her hand from her wound, wetting my fingers in the blood. Slowly, I dragged my fingers down her stomach, leaving long lines on her pale skin. Again, I collected more blood, slowing the movement of the knife. I circled her clit with my bloodied fingers, my need for her growing as her breathing quickened.

I undid my pants, pulling myself free. Her eyes widened briefly at the sight of me, her hips lifting and grinding into the knife handle.

"You want this?" I murmured, rubbing myself against her clit.

She closed her eyes, tipping her head back. "Yes," she whispered.

I removed the knife, rubbed my hand in her blood, and stroked myself with it. "Beg for me." Her face screwed up, a mixture of discomfort and disgust creasing her features. I leaned closer to her, applying pressure to her clit. "Beg," I growled, wiping my hand off on the pale grey carpet.

Her voice, tiny but firm, whimpered out, "Fuck me, please."

"Louder." I rubbed against her, teasing her.

She moaned, trying to grind herself against me. "Please, fuck me."

Thrusting into her, I gripped her hips and pulled her roughly against me. "Very polite. I'll fix that." I lifted her legs onto my shoulders and pounded into her. She cried out, digging her fingers into the carpet, trying to brace herself. Soft moans escaped her lips, her face flushing as I moved inside her. The moans of pleasure quickly began to dissolve into grunts and cries of pain. I stopped and rolled her over, her back red and raw from rubbing against the carpet.

Guilt knotted in my stomach. I reached my hand to try to soothe the wound, but the whirling sound of the camera on the wall stopped me. *He's watching...*

"On your knees."

Leaning on her forearms, she knelt with her ass in the air before me. I grabbed a fist full of her hair, pulling her head back. "Good girl," I growled into her ear, plunging myself back in. She gasped, an explicit tumbling from her lips. I fucked her harder, a low guttural groan escaping my throat as I realized she was matching my pace. I released her hair and pulled out.

She turned suddenly, taking me into her mouth, tasting herself on me with long strokes of her tongue. Slowly her lips wrapped around my cock as she swallowed me, locking eyes with me as though accepting the challenge.

"Oh, fuck—" I exploded down her throat, holding her head against me as I came. She sucked me as she leaned back, wiping her swollen lips on the back of her hand.

I stared at her dumbfounded. She straightened, pushing her hair from her face, and smiled coyly at me. "Stand up," I said, sitting back. She stood, and I looked her over, motioning her to turn around. Her forearms, knees, and back were red with rug burn. The wound on her shoulder had stopped bleeding, but the blood was all over her arm, stomach, and thighs. I glanced at the carpet, smirking at the stains.

I stood, tucking a stray hair behind her ear. "You didn't come," I whispered. She shivered, leaning closer to me.

The door slammed open, and Priscilla's crooked frame stalked through the door. "What have we here? A whole room dedicated to training, and I find you in here?" She clicked her tongue at me before marching over to Belle, taking her by the chin. "I see why Gaston chose you."

Belle's eyes widened, ticking to me and back to Priscilla as the woman grabbed her by the arm and forced her to spin around.

I pulled my pants up and fastened them. "What are you doing here, Priscilla?" I went to roll my sleeves up but thought better of it and folded my arms.

"Checking in that you boys are doing your job and not just playing." She took something out from her pocket, a small vial containing a clear liquid. She grabbed Belle's hair, twisting her head back. Belle opened her mouth to scream, and Priscilla poured the liquid into her mouth.

I caught Belle as she stumbled away from the woman, coughing and choking on the mystery liquid. "What the fuck was that?" I demanded, lowering Belle to the ground as her body went limp.

Priscilla scowled. "Oh, interesting. Not quite the effect I was hoping for." She pocketed the vial and made her way to the door. "Keep an eye on her. I'd like to know how it reacts over the next few hours." She glanced back at us, sighed in annoyance, and slipped out the door.

After dressing Belle, I sat with her until she started to wake up, and then I took her back to the cell.

Nine

Belle

"Sh... I think she's waking up." Voices whispered near me, shuffling around. My head was throbbing right behind my eyes. I peeked with one eye, finding the room dim, only a dim light bulb hanging from the ceiling casting any light.

I sat up slowly, the cold, hard floor having made my body sore and stiff. Ella stirred next to me, gently caressing my cheek. "You're awake," she whispered, dropping her hand to her lap.

"Were you talking to someone?" I rubbed my temples, trying to ease the pressure.

She shook her head, swiping away a long, light strand of

hair from her eyes. "No one else in here but us," she said, scooting closer. "Are you okay?"

"I think so..." I mumbled, noticing movement in the back of the room. I turned toward it, the motion causing a tinge of pain to jolt through my hips. I winced, readjusting myself.

Ella picked at her fingernails, drawing her bottom lip between her teeth. "You were gone for a while. I got worried something happened to you."

I took her hand and squeezed it, trying to think of something reassuring to say when, again, I noticed something move, and a voice whispered, "She could be the one to break the curse." I squinted at the darkness. In the corner, a spoon and fork huddled.

"Oh, holy... Are you seeing this?" I glanced at Ella and pointed at the cutlery.

The spoon gasped as the fork jumped in front of her. "Don't hurt us! We're trapped in here, just like you. Cursed to spend eternity in this form."

I startled, bumping into Ella, causing a sharp pain to shoot through my arm. "Oh shit," I gasped, memories of what had happened outside the room rushing back to me.

Ella looked from the corner to me, her blue eyes wide.

"There's nothing there, Belle... Are you okay?"

The fork was begging me to help now, and the spoon began crying. I shifted away, my arm screaming in pain as my clothing rubbed against it. "You don't see the fork and spoon talking about curses?" I grimaced. "The spoon is crying."

"Oh, fuck... What did he give you?" Ella placed her hands on both sides of my face and leaned in, looking at my eyes.

A flicker of memory broke through the brain fog. "Not him. Priscilla. She made me drink something... I can't remember..." My head pounded when I tried to think about it, making me dizzy and nauseous.

"Hopefully, it'll wear off soon..." She let me go, and I shivered, a cold sweat beading up on my brow. She wrapped her arm around me, and I tensed as she rubbed against some of my fresh wounds. "There's no spoon or fork over there. Just try to relax and enjoy the trip."

The fork hopped across the room and stood before us. "Madam, *please*," he begged, "just listen to what we have to say."

I looked from the hallucination to Ella. "Are you sure?" I whispered, clinging to the thin fabric of her shirt. "They're talking about a curse..."

She pulled my head to her shoulder, combing her fingers through my hair, pushing it from my face. "I'm positive. The only curse is that we are locked in this room."

Closing my eyes, I tried to ignore the cutlery, crying for my attention. I was drifting off to sleep when the door slammed open. Ella held me tighter as she spoke to the man standing in the doorway. My vision wavered, and everything they said sounded like it was being yelled down a tunnel.

The brightness of the hall light turned the man into a show creature, wrapping his tendrils around Ella's limbs and ripped her from my arms. I scrambled to grasp a hold of her again, but he was faster than I was in my altered state. He shut off the light above me. By the time I looked from the light back to the creature, the door slammed shut. The darkness enveloped me like a prickly, frozen wool blanket. I curled up into myself, careful not to bump any of my new wounds. Not even the hallucinations bothered to keep me company in the dark.

I drifted in and out of sleep, the concrete floor causing a chill through my body. I struggled to find warmth from anything, tucking my arms in my clothing and pressing myself against the wall. The effects of whatever Priscilla was beginning to fade when the door opened again.

"Get up."

The light turned on, making my head pound. I groaned, throwing my arm over my eyes, and attempted to stand. Suddenly, I was being hoisted up, an arm snaking under mine and around my back for support. The skull mask hovered beside my face, blurring in and out of my peripheral vision as we moved from the room.

I leaned heavily against him, his sweatshirt brushing against my cheek. "I feel strange," I mumbled as we entered a room with a bed. The Beast helped me into the bed, pressing the back of his hand against my forehead.

"The bitch is gone. Get some rest. We'll continue when it's out of your system." He rolled his sleeve up as he turned, and I caught a glimpse of a shadow wolf on his bicep before falling asleep.

Ten

Adam

With a cigarette clenched between my teeth, I paced the large wooden deck facing the dense forest in Gaston's mansion's backyard. I was at my breaking point. I needed a plan, something to get Belle and myself out of this mess. The way she looked after whatever Priscilla forced down her throat made my blood boil. Killing Gaston wouldn't be sufficient; Priscilla would also need to be taken down simultaneously. That way, all the blackmail they had on Chris and I wouldn't be released...

Pressing the call button for a third time, I turned and leaned against the railing as the phone rang.

On the third ring, the ringtone abruptly cut off to a brief

crackle of static. Scattered voices shouted above techno music in the background. "One second." A deep voice snarled, followed by a door slamming and silence. "Adam, this better be fuckin' important! I'm *workin'*."

I quickly moved down the steps and began jogging away from the house. "Is Akari safe?" I asked, knowing the question would simmer Fenrir's mood and pique his curiosity.

There was a beat of silence as the question sank in. "I have eyes on her. What are you gettin' at, bub?"

Stopping a good distance away from the house, I took a drag of my cigarette. "Gaston's got my balls in a vice, Fen. He an' Priscilla got some kind of plan that involves Akari and framing me to get you pissed. Fucker doesn't realize you an' I hashed our differences."

Fenrir snorted, a dark chuckle rumbling across the line. "Who'd he hire?"

"Fuck if I know. I'm just givin' you a heads up. I ain't playin' this shit. I'm good at my job for a reason, and he's about to find out firsthand." I ground my cigarette against a tree trunk and dropped it.

"Take him out, and that will make you...?" he trailed off, amusement lifting his voice.

I smirked, starting back toward the house. "Not sure yet, Fen. This business is tainted."

He made a sound of approval, the background noise suddenly starting again. "I'll put out some extra eyes. I got a lake house... Text Thomas Boots when you're done. Keys are under the water drain." He hung up, and I pocketed my phone as I made my way inside.

Belle was still asleep two hours after I moved her to a bedroom. Her fever had at least broken, and the color seemed to be returning to her face. I'd play along for the hidden cameras until I had a solid plan in line. After that conversation with Fenrir and the potential mics in the woods, it needed to be soon.

I shot Chris a text:

I'm out of Jack and Coke.

I hated the drink. It was our code to have a conversation outside of Gaston and Priscilla's reach. We'd been talking potential takeover for years... This was our chance.

I placed my phone on the nightstand next to a glass of water and a sandwich I had made for her. With my mask in place, I nudged her awake. "Time to get up, darlin'."

She sat straight up with a gasp, her hands clutching at the blanket beneath her.

Moving to the foot of the bed, I held my hands up. "Relax. You're safe." I motioned to the food and drink on the nightstand.

Her shoulders slumped slightly, and her eyes flicked from the food to me. "Safe..." she mumbled dryly, glaring at me through the mess of hair that had fallen in front of her face. Brushing it to the side, she grabbed the glass of water and downed it.

"If I'm safe... then tell me who you are."

I smirked, watching her take the sandwich and take a bite. "If you didn't believe me, then why are you eating?" I countered.

She paused mid-chew and looked down at the sandwich. "Touché." She snorted and continued to eat. "Why didn't you tell me you kidnapped me for Gaston?"

Tipping my head toward the camera in the room, I shrugged. "I did."

Rolling her eyes, she finished the last bite of her sandwich and brushed her hands off on her jeans. "Can I at least see your face?" she asked, watching me stalk to her side.

"No. Take your clothes off and get in the shower."

She stared at me for a long moment, then nodded. As she walked to the bathroom, she stripped naked, revealing swollen wounds across her shoulder blades and upper back. She pulled the frosted door to the side, turned the water on, and stepped inside.

"Would you like to join me?" she called out, making me laugh.

I leaned against the door frame, watching her blurry silhouette lather soap into her hair. "So you can see my face?"

"I want to confirm my suspicions."

My clothes were beginning to feel tight. I wanted to climb into the hot spray of water with her. Swallowing thickly, I asked, "What are your suspicions?"

My phone chirped behind me, Chris' tone. When Belle didn't respond, I grabbed it and checked the new message.

> *Fuck your Jack and Coke. I'm not your bartended*

I rolled my eyes and sent a rose emoji, then the text:

> *BartendeR. I'm going fishing tonight at 8. I'll get the booze later.*

Before I could even set my phone down, Chris responded:

> *Fuck u. Have fun.*

He was so fucking thick-skulled sometimes. At least I knew where he was staying tonight if he didn't catch on by 7:30.

The shower turned off, and Belle wandered into the room wrapped in a black towel. She stared at me, her hair dripping in her face. "I'm done."

Eleven

Belle

THE BRAIN FOG LIFTED as I showered, the heat soothing the aches and pains littered across my body. Rust-colored water ran down my legs and circled the drain. I lathered with the bar of soap, scrubbing the rest of the dry blood from my stomach and thighs. Pieces of memory clicked into place as I rinsed my hair. The ringtone was the last piece I needed.

The tone sparked a memory from a night at Adam's apartment. I had heard the sound that chimed from the other room that night. Adam ignored it at first. His cell phone was programmed with different ringtones and sounds, so he knew which to ignore. After the tenth notification, he apologized, untangled himself from me, and picked up the phone with a muttered curse. *"Fuck, Chris can be so impatient."*

I had my suspicions that the monster in the other room was Adam when he pressed me against the wall and said he'd been hired. The familiarity of him hit all at once. His body language, the way he touched me, his smell, his cock... The tattoo on his bicep and the ringtone for his best friend...

It was him.

And he wanted me to know. At least, I was hoping that was the case and not some sick game he was playing. I didn't want to believe he had been corrupted by Gaston's darkness. He was far from pure, but evil had never been a vibe I felt from him.

I grabbed the black towel hanging beside the shower and got out. Adam lifted his head as I entered the room and stopped beside the bed. Standing before him, naked and vulnerable, I tried to wrap my mind around why he would kidnap me... and for Gaston of all people. Anger swelled in my stomach until he nervously glanced at the corner of the room again. Following his gaze, I noticed a small object mounted at the top of the wall.

Another camera... He had warned me about a camera in the last room as well. This is an act... It has to be...

He grabbed me, ripped the towel from my body, and tossed it on the bed. "I still owe you," he growled in my ear, letting his eyes roam over my exposed breasts.

"He's watching, isn't he?" I whispered, allowing him to shove me on the bed, forcing me on my knees. I heard his zipper and the shuffling of his pants being removed. I peeked over my shoulder at him, butterflies exploding in my stomach at the sight of his cock.

Stroking himself as he stepped closer to me. "Talk, and you'll be punished." His deep, husky voice sent sparks through my body. I wanted to be on top, his hands massaging my breasts as I rode him to completion inside me. I wanted to be wet with his seed...

"Punished?" As soon as the word spilled from my mouth, he slapped my butt. I yelped and bit my lip to keep from saying anything else.

He ran his hand over where he hit me, easing the sting. I moaned as his fingers parted me, and he rubbed himself against me. "Be a good girl and shut up," he said huskily, the tip of his cock circling my clit. My eyes rolled back at the sensation, and I lifted my hips, trying to feel more of him. He slid his cock back and slowly entered me. Once he was halfway in, he thrust forward, earning a moan from me. He gripped my hips, his fingernails digging into my flesh as he rocked inside me.

Panting, I tried to match his movement, snaking my hand between my legs.

He stopped abruptly and smacked my butt again. The sound shocked me more than the pain. "Did I say you could touch yourself?" I dropped my hand to the bed, glaring at him over my shoulder. He narrowed his eyes at me. "Don't touch yourself unless I say so," he ordered, fisting my hair and pulling my head back. The fangs from his mask brushed against the edge of my ear. "Scream." His voice rasped through the teeth of the skull as he slammed into me.

I cried out, overplaying discomfort, squirming as though the feeling of his hand in my hair hurt. He pulled harder, and I screamed louder, resisting the urge to say his name. I dug my fingers into the bedding, clutching at the fabric as he pounded against my cervix. My head fell forward as he released my hair and raked his nails down my back, carefully avoiding the rug burn. I whimpered, arching my back into his hand.

"Fuck," he growled, pulling me onto his lap, grinding into me. "I won't let him fuckin' touch you," he mumbled, running his hands over my breasts and stomach, sliding down between my thighs. "You're fuckin' mine."

The words sent chills up my spine. "Yes," I breathed out, bouncing on him, leaning against his chest as he explored my body.

His fingers wrapped around my neck, applying slight pressure, making my head swim. "Beast..." I panted, needing to say something to acknowledge him but afraid to say his name out loud. It was something I had heard his friend refer to him as. With the mask on, it felt fitting. "Harder, Beast."

He moved us, so I was back on my knees again. He shoved my face down into the pillows and rammed into me. I bit into the pillow, my screams muffled as he ravaged me.

"Touch yourself for me," he grunted, slowing just enough that I could push up onto my forearms.

Not needing to be told twice, I found my clit and rubbed. My legs trembled, the heat in my core spreading through my body. He teased my right nipple, pinching and pulling it. My toes curled at the sensation. As I hit my peak, he quickened his pace, and I screamed, my body shaking in ecstasy. He pulled out from me and flipped me over, pumping his cock and releasing thick streams across my chest and face.

"Fuck," he groaned, handing me the towel from my shower, and wandered into the bathroom. "Clean up. I need to return you to the cell."

Twelve

Adam

THE CELL WAS EMPTY when I returned Belle to it. In the darkness, I lifted my mask and pressed my lips against hers. Her mouth eagerly opened for me, allowing me to explore. I broke away, lowering the mask, and turned the bulb on for her. "I'll come back."

She grabbed my hand, pulling my arm straight. Her fingers traced alone where my shadow wolf tattoo was underneath my sweatshirt. "Next time... I want to see the tattoo," she whispered, her eyes snapping up to mine. "No mask, Beast."

I chuckled. "No mask, little rabbit."

My phone rang, breaking the comfortable silence between

us. *Gaston*. I cursed, leaving the cell, and locked the door behind me. "Yeah?" I answered, making my way up the stairs and toward the backyard for a smoke.

"Adam, I have a mission for you," Gaston's annoyingly arrogant voice hollered through the phone, aggressive techno music playing in the background. "I need you to take care of someone for me. It'll take you two days."

I froze, my heart slamming against my ribs. "What about the girl?" I fished out my pack of cigarettes, shoving one in my mouth.

"Two days alone will be great torture. She'll be fawning all over me when I arrive. Which"—he chuckled to himself, amused with whatever scenario he had made up in his mind— "I shall be arriving the day after you return from your mission. Make sure she's not dead. Give her some stale bread, so she has energy for me."

The cigarette snapped between my teeth. "Who am I offing, Gaston?" I ground out, spitting the broken pieces off the side of the deck. I stuck a fresh one between my lips and lit it, taking a long drag.

Gaston sighed, an exaggerated sound as though he were hamming it up for some audience. "Jaq, Gustav's brother. You see... Gustav is proving to be a thorn in my side. He needs a gentle reminder of who is in charge."

I blew smoke out at the grey sky. "Offing his brother is going to be that gentle reminder?"

"You know what the man's hobbies are, Beast?" Gaston's voice turned dark, the jovial tone replaced with a husky low rumble. "You all seem to mistake him for the horny sonofabitch that likes to go through women like god damned toilet paper. But the man is vying for the position of the Devil, Adam. You hear me? Those women are nothing but sport. The man owns an island off the west coast where he kidnaps the neighboring locals and sets them free. For a mere couple thousand, you can hunt them. For a few grand more, he turns your catch into trophies." His tone lifted suddenly, "Like lamps and leather tapestries."

"That's gross, Gaston," I grumbled. I could have gone my whole life without knowing any of the information he just spilled. "So... ending Jaq will remind Gustav that you're worse than that?" I put out my cigarette and stalked through the house to the front.

"Indeed. Jaq will be making an appearance in New Orleans tonight. He's buying a lot of inventory. I have men waiting to swoop in to relocate it after you complete your mission." He laughed, and for a moment, I heard Louis joining in only to abruptly with a moan.

My skin crawled. I shuddered, holding the phone away

from my ear as more sounds began picking up. "Coordinates?" I asked, climbing into my car.

Gaston breathily rattled off an address and time. "Good boy," he moaned, and I hung up, trying to erase the entire phone call from my mind except what I needed to know.

I'd be driving most of the night to get there. That meant I'd have to book a hotel for two nights, but that would give me plenty of time to scout the area where I'd be finding Jaq. I texted Chris I'd be out of town, to make sure Belle got food and water, and to forget the Jack and Coke. About an hour later, I received a message from him.

What the fuck are you on?

I was going to give him a whole fucking earful about remembering code words when I got back. Cranking up the radio, I rolled down the window and lit a cigarette.

I made good time. The eight-hour drive only took me six. I parked at a nearby motel and stopped in a pub for a beer and burger. After that, I went back to the motel and crashed for the night.

The next afternoon, I explored the area, checking out where Jaq was supposed to arrive later. To my surprise, the man was already there, barking out orders to a few mousy-looking boys. He was a tall, lanky man with a scraggily beard and ripped dirty sweats. No way in the world would I have ever pegged him for having millions.

Ducking into a nearby oddities store selling alligator heads, I spied out the front window as I pretended to be interested in the crystal collection sitting on a table. I wanted to slit the man's throat now and be done with it, but word would get back to Gaston, and being so far from Belle...

Jaq hopped into a white van, and I exited the store as it

drove off. A few kids scattered about, closing up the garage doors before climbing into a car and heading in the same direction as the van.

Curious, I tested the garage door. It lifted with barely any effort. I rolled my eyes, slid it halfway open, and crouched under. Using my phone as a flashlight, I peered around. The place was already half full of large cardboard boxes marked "fragile." One was left opened, the flaps sticking straight in the air. I peeked inside, discovering vials similar to the one Priscilla had.

"The fuck is going on..." I mumbled, taking a vile and pocketed it. I scanned the area once more and left, locking the garage to avoid any potential surveillance cameras being checked when Jaq discovered it wasn't secured.

I found a bar with a football game on to waste the remainder of my time in. I ordered a beer and took it to a booth in the far corner. Once settled, I called Fenrir to give him a heads-up.

"Beast... It's unusual you call me this often," Fenrir answered, his voice tinged with curiosity.

I casually looked about the room, making sure no one was within earshot of me. "It'll be quick. I have info."

"I'm listening."

"Priscilla is working with the rat brothers. She has some kind of drug she's working on. Not sure what it's meant for, but I just discovered Jaq with a shit ton in his possession. Not only that, but Gaston is about to snipe it from him tonight after Jaq has an unfortunate accident. I grabbed a sample for you."

Fenrir hummed. "Gaston hired you for a hit on Jaq?"

"Yep." I took a drink from my mug, frowning at the score on the TV.

"Curious. Why?"

I lowered my eyes to the waitress approaching and waved her off. She smiled politely at me and went back to the counter. "He said to put Gustav in line. He's been overstepping. Didn't really say anything else."

"It's been noticed. Thank you, friend." Fenrir hung up, and I pocketed my phone, waving to the waitress.

She perked up and sauntered over. "What can I get ya, sugah?" she asked, tapping her ruby-red lips with the end of her pen.

I smiled. "Basket of fries and another beer."

"Got it." She winked at me, sashaying her perfectly round ass as she wandered back to the kitchen. My cock twitched, memories of my morning with Belle rushing through my mind. I groaned, downing my beer. It was going to be a long day.

Thirteen

Belle

THE AIR WAS HEAVY with the horrid smell of bodily fluids... I huddled close to Ella, the temperature feeling as though it were dropping by the minute. Our breaths came out in small puffs of white clouds, disappearing into the darkness.

It'd been a few hours since Adam locked me back in the cell with the promise of returning. My insides twisted with worry, fear, and anger. Despite everything that'd happened, I'd only ever known Adam to be honest with me.

"We can't stay here," I whispered, Ella burying her hands between us to warm her fingers. "I gotta find a way out."

"How?" Ella rasped, her body trembling with a sudden

shudder. "They've got eyes everywhere, and Chris..." Her voice hitched as she trailed off.

I found her hands, intertwining my fingers with hers. "We're smarter than them. We'll watch, wait... strike when they least expect it."

She squeezed my hand, another shiver wracking through her body. "What if we're stuck here forever?" The words spilled from her lips, fear lacing them. "What about life outside these walls, dreams, family..."

"Shh." I brushed my thumb across her knuckle. "Don't let them take what's yours, Ella. Hold on to it, fight for it." I had half a mind to tell her that I recognized Adam, but the longer the minutes ticked by, the more I second-guessed my trust in him.

Ella buried her face into my shoulder, her breath warming my skin through my shirt. I held her to me, rubbing her arm in a vain attempt to soothe the nightmares running rampant in her mind. I kissed the top of her head, murmuring words of encouragement, hoping they weren't going unheard. Hoping they would come to fruition and Adam would be back with a plan...

Our moment shattered as the door's lock clicked. Chris's silhouette filled the doorway, huge and menacing. Ella tensed against me, her head lifting from my shoulder as

Chris stepped into the room.

"Time to split up, lovelies," Priscilla's grating voice cut through like nails on a chalkboard as she followed Chris inside. Market day is coming, and we need you both looking your best. You, Ella, have a very special buyer, and you need to undergo the proper training. Such an exciting day, isn't it, girls?"

I squeezed Ella's hand, not willing to let her go without a fight. Our eyes met. She swallowed hard and turned to them. "You can't sell us," she declared with venom in her voice. Pride flooded through me.

Priscilla cackled, high, and raspy like I pictured the witch would sound in my favorite fairytale. "Watch me." She crept closer, her long, gnarly finger pointed at us. "Ella, to your new quarters. Chris will escort you."

Chris moved forward, his boots scraping against the cement floor. I gritted my teeth, searching for the strength and courage Ella just exhibited. I wanted to protect her too. I wanted to be strong like the heroes in my books.

"Time to move," Chris demanded, his voice cutting through me like ice. I moved to stand, to make a bold statement like Ella just had. To demand they both let us go or... or... He chuckled, breaking me of my thoughts. "Not you. Just her. Someone else is coming for you, *princess.*"

My voice escaped me as Ella used my arm to stand, her legs shaking beneath her. She let go of my hand, and I reached for her but missed as she stepped out of my reach. The coldness of the room hit harder than it ever had, sinking into my bones and making my teeth clatter.

"Walk," Chris ordered, his voice a guttural rumble.

Ella steadily moved away from me, her feet dragging on the ground. I wanted to run to her, to pull her back to the safety of our corner... but my legs gave out, and I sunk to the floor, curling in on myself as Chris's cold gray eyes flickered to me and back to Ella. There was something in them as they landed on her, a softness. His whole body shifted as though he were protecting her from something. It was fleeting, but I held hope that it meant he was on the same page as Adam... That this fate Priscilla and Gaston had in mind for us was not what they planned on fulfilling.

"Move it, little ember," Chris mumbled, his hand moving to the small of her back and hovered.

Ella froze, her body swaying like a leaf in the wind. She lowered her head, her shoulders rising to her ears.

"Didn't hear me?" Chris roughly grabbed her arm.

"Let go!" Ella tried to jerk away, but Chris held tight, unmoving.

"Easy there," he drawled, dragging her to the door. "Wouldn't want to bruise the goods."

Goods. That's all we were to them. A product to be bartered, broken, sold... Rage bubbled up, hot and fierce, but I choked it down. If I had an outburst, it could mean death to either of us. We needed to be smart to survive.

Priscilla's heels noisily clicked out of the room after Chris and Ella. She didn't say a word to me as she slammed the door shut. "Fuck you," I mumbled under my breath. "You'll get yours. You *and* Gaston."

Fourteen

Adam

To my extreme irritation, Jaq didn't show up. I waited nearly all night for him to return and ended up back at the motel at around 4 in the morning. I called Gaston, not giving a fuck about the time.

I shouldn't have been surprised when the man answered, sounding as though he were at the bar. "Beast! How's it going?"

"He didn't show, Gaston. What's the deal?" I growled, shoving a cigarette between my teeth.

"No? Oh, my bad. I meant he'd be there early in the morning... today actually! Lucky you!" He laughed, shouting to the bartender for another round of drinks. "The rest of the shipment was set to arrive by 7 AM this morning. He should be there before then, but I recommend waiting for the truck to leave before... well, *you* know!"

I made to hang up when I heard him ask, "Have you heard from Chris by any chance?"

"No." I scowled, removing my cigarette from my mouth. I tapped my fingers on my thigh, waiting for him to divulge why he was asking about Chris.

Glasses clinked nearby, followed by a cheer. Gaston chuckled softly. "Interesting. Seems your bestie took off with Gustav's purchase sometime a day or two ago. Priscilla is *very* upset." He enunciated the last sentence, amusement lacing his voice. "I'm thrilled. It's like killing two birds with one stone. Both are furious and out searching for them. Gustav is paying double for *both* now. Something about wanting Chris to enjoy his island. Priscilla decided she'd stay at the mansion with her security, keeping watch until her men find Chris."

"Neat," I grunted, rubbing my temple. "Do you need anything else from me?"

Gaston hummed, rumbling in laughter. "You? No. Enjoy your night, Beast." He hung up, and I realized I was clenching my jaw so hard that it was beginning to ache.

Fuck! If Chris is gone... Then that means no one is helping Belle... My stomach dropped at the thought. I had my suspicions that Gaston paid off Jaq's employees, meaning he probably had eyes around the city waiting for me to take him out.

I dialed Chris' phone, cursing under my breath when it went to voicemail. I tried his burner phone. He answered before the first ring even had a chance to finish. "Adam," he whispered.

"I have news."

"Make it quick," he said in the same hushed tone.

I lit my cigarette and took a drag. "Gaston knows you've taken Ella and ran. Gustav and Priscilla are after your heads. Priscilla is staying at the mansion with upped security while their men search for you. Keep moving. I'm heading back in the morning and only have this phone since my trip was unexpected."

"Get rid of it," he commanded. "Now. Use the burner. I'll be in touch."

"I'll be dumping it on my way back. I need it for now. Gaston is my next target. Fenrir has offered his lake house to us."

"Understood," he said before hanging up.

I napped and arrived at the location a little after seven. By noon, there still was no truck. I left to get lunch and call Gaston. The asshole didn't bother answering my call, instead texted me a barely coherent text about keeping watch. Every other word was misspelled or abbreviated.

It was around seven that *night* when the shipment finally came in. Gaston was never off on his times, and the fact that he was not only once but twice only gave me more motivation to shove my hunting knife through his eye.

As I had suspected, Gaston had managed to pay off Jaq's employees. I discovered this when Jaq returned to the garage, and the group of five working with him conveniently disappeared. He noticed a moment too late.

I slit his throat, and he lurched forward, grasping the gaping wound. Twisting to face me, his face quickly paling, he reached for me. I backed up a step, watching him fall to his knees, drawing in wet, raspy gasps. I plunged the knife into his chest. He grabbed my hand and held it with the last of his energy, blood spilling from his mouth over my knuckles.

I left his body in the garage and cleaned up in the bathroom of a shady bar nearby. Not one person even looked up when I walked through. Everyone was perfectly content minding their own business, shooting pool, and enjoying their beer and popcorn. I contemplated having a beer, but thoughts of Belle had me rushing back to the motel.

After showering and trying to clean my pants of as much blood as I could, I called Gaston to report in. He answered on the third ring by singing my name over the roar of the bar. "Beasty! How is your night going?"

"Job's done." I rubbed my eyes, sitting on the edge of the bed, waiting for him to dismiss me so I could get some sleep before my drive in the morning. I really wanted to drive through the night to get back to Belle... especially since she'd been in the cell for at least forty-eight hours at this point. Guilt twisted my stomach at the thought. Chris being on the run meant no one was there to help her, except maybe Priscilla. *That* thought brought bile up in my throat. But I'd be no help to her dead if I crashed falling asleep...

"Yeah, yeah, I was told. Glad to have that fucker out of the way. Hated looking at that ugly face of his." Gaston heaved a heavy sigh as though it was something that had been sitting on his shoulders for a long time.

I held the phone with my shoulder against my ear. "You had me kill him because you thought he was ugly?" I tapped my pack of cigarettes against my palm, finding two left inside.

Without hesitation, Gaston blurted out, "Yes." He laughed, the sound making me irrationally angry. "I'll add a little extra to your next paycheck." The call ended, and I exhaled in a loud burst. I set an alarm for three hours and promptly passed out in exhaustion.

I was now twenty minutes away from home, out of cigs,

and annoyed about the blood stain on my jeans. I had to tie my hoodie around my waist to get gas to hide it, feeling like a moron the entire time. My phone lit up in the cup holder, and Gaston's name scrawled across the screen.

I answered, grunting out a quick, "Yeah?"

Gaston said something quickly, the wind from my open window causing a roaring static over his stupid voice.

"Hold on, I didn't hear you," I yelled over the noise, rolling my window up.

"Fuck are you doing, mutt?" Gaston snarled. "I don't have fucking time for your shit."

My eyebrows shot up at the aggression in his voice, and immediately, concern for Belle rushed through my blood. "I'm on my way back to the house."

Heavy footfalls echoed in the background, and his voice took on a similar tone as though he'd walked into a garage. "Shit is going on at the house. I'm collecting Belle once it quiets. Your mission is complete. Go home and wait for me to contact you again." He hung up without waiting for me to respond.

I quickly called Chris, my call going to voicemail without even ringing. "Fuck!" I shouted, glancing at my phone to call him again, but noticed a text message sent a couple of hours earlier.

> *Hopefully you fucking listened and got rid of this, but if not. I'm confronting the cunt. See ya on the beach.*

I deleted all my messages, rolled down my window, and dropped the phone out. In my rearview mirror, I watched a semi-truck roll over it, pieces scattering across the cement.

The bodies behind the bushes weren't hard to miss, especially with the stench. *Fuck, Chris... discrete never was your thing.*

I hurried past more bodies, and blood splattered to the cells. Somewhere upstairs, in the maze of corridors, I could hear shouts and screams. *Nice, Chris..., he must still be settling business.* I had faith he wouldn't leave any stones unturned as I made it to Belle's prison cell and yanked open the door.

Curled up in a tight little ball in the corner of the room, Belle lay. My heart dropped at the sight of her, and I rushed in, fearing she was dead. "Belle!"

She stirred, lifting her head as I scooped her up in my arms. "Fuck, I'm so sorry," I whispered, hurrying out of the room with her.

"Adam?" she whispered, her voice hoarse and raspy.

"Yeah, babe, it's me. Don't talk, just rest." Screaming picked up again on the other side of the mansion, followed by objects breaking. I went in the opposite direction, heading into the large kitchen that overlooked the backyard. Helping Belle into a chair, I made sure she was steady before throwing open cupboards until I found a glass and filled it with water. "I'm sorry! I'm so sorry!" I blurted out, handing her the glass.

She drank it down greedily, water spilling out the corner of her lips. I grabbed another glass and filled it, setting it on the table for her. She set the empty cup down and picked up the other, holding it as she caught her breath.

"I'm going to make you some food," I said, rummaging

through the refrigerator for something quick to put together.

Belle set the second glass down, half empty, and wiped her mouth on her shoulder. "Where were you?" She leaned her forearms against her thighs, watching me put together a sandwich for her.

"Gaston sent me on a wild goose chase of a fuckin' job. I didn't expect Chris to take off at the same time." I handed her the turkey and cheese sandwich, went back to the fridge, and pulled open drawers for something else to give her.

Fifteen

Belle

Adam turned back to me, peeling an orange. His eyebrows creased together as I scarfed down the sandwich, barely tasting it. Nearly three days alone in that room, no food, no water... I thought I was going to die. I had just given up on the idea that someone was going to save me when he returned.

The screaming on the other side of the house quieted, replaced with the occasional moan. I finished the sandwich, trying to ignore the obvious sounds of sex. Adam's face screwed up as he realized what we were hearing as well. "Guess they're having all the fun," he muttered, handing me the orange. "Can I get you anything else?"

I pulled off sections of the orange, eating them slower than I had the sandwich. The lightheaded feeling was finally beginning to fade. "No..." I lifted my eyes to his. "I thought you left me for dead," I admitted, biting into the fruit and enjoying the sweetness of it flooding my mouth.

"I'm sorry." He pressed his hands on the counter and leaned forward, the muscles in his forearms flexing under his weight. "I should have brought you with me."

Finishing up the orange, I wiped my hands on my pants. "You couldn't, right? Just like they couldn't let me out before fucking in the other room. I'm fucking disposable." The words flooded from me with vitriol.

"You're not."

"The fuck I'm not! Everyone left me there alone in a dark room to die!" Cries of pleasure interrupted me. I rolled my eyes, wiping the tears from my face with the back of my wrist. "Of all the people, I didn't expect you to hurt me like that," I muttered.

For a moment, I regretted my words. Shakily, I looked up at him, expecting anger and a defense. Instead, we locked eyes, and Adam exhaled a long, slow breath.

He raked his hands through his hair. "I deserved that." He sighed, scratching at the back of his neck before shoving his hands in his pockets restlessly. "I'm sorry. I know that's not enough... What you went through... That'll never be enough. But I hope to make it right and earn your trust again."

I nodded, at a sudden loss of words. We sat in silence, listening to Ella and Chris on the other side of the mansion. The kitchen was beginning to close in on me.

"What now? Any plans?" I asked, popping another section of orange in my mouth, and pressed my feet against the cold floor tiles.

"Need to get you cleaned up." Adam glanced down at the dark red stains on his jeans. "And me... We can head back to my apartment. You can at least shower, and I'll try to get you something clean to wear. But we'll need to be quick."

A door opened somewhere, and I could hear Ella's soft voice dancing down the hall mixed with Chris's. The two giggled, exiting out the front door, not even realizing we were right there in the kitchen. They didn't even bother to check if I was still in the cell. My heart ached, a mixture of hurt and happiness that she was safe, at least.

Adam's face shifted from annoyed to amused and back to sober as his eyes rested on me. "Are you okay?"

The question seemed so absurd I almost laughed. I shook

my head. "A shower sounds nice," I whispered, standing. The room spun briefly, and I dropped back to the chair.

He moved to my side. "Take it easy... Let me help you." He wrapped his arm under my armpits and lifted me to my feet, allowing me to lean against him as my legs shook.

"I'll be okay. It just... It was a long few days. I'm exhausted." I swallowed thickly, trying to dislodge the emotions sitting heavily on my chest. I wanted to scream, cry, fight someone... For the first time in my life, I wanted to drown my despair with alcohol, hoping the memories would vanish one day.

Adam hugged me to him. "I'm sorry, little rabbit. I'll make it up to you."

Adam

BELLE FELL ASLEEP ALMOST as soon as she sat down. Her body trembled, and she mumbled incoherently in her sleep. Minutes before we reached my apartment, she woke up and stared quietly out her window.

I opened her door for her, and she got out, the shaking barely noticeable. I wrapped my arm around her protectively, leading her to my second-floor apartment.

She took everything in, a slow smile working its way across her beautiful face. "Some things never change," she said, making her way to the bathroom. "I'll be quick."

I bit my lip, resisting the urge to join her. *Next time.* "New toothbrushes are in the middle drawer!" I called after her as I passed the bathroom to my room.

I busied myself in my closet, pulling out a screen print

T-shirt with a wolf on it. The shirt was silly, but Belle...
she could make a tablecloth work. Pants were harder, but
I found a pair of jeans from when I was in high school that
had tagged along with me for some reason. They were too
small for me, but they looked like they would easily fit her,
or at least would with a belt. I fished out a pair of sandals
and made a mental note to include shoes when we bought
her new clothes.

Setting the ensemble on the bed, I pulled out my duffel bag
and began shoving clothes inside. On the top shelf of my
closet, I grabbed a box and opened it, finding my stash of
emergency cash and a burner phone. I put it all in the front
pocket of my bag and zipped everything shut, setting it by
the front door.

When I turned around, Belle was standing in the hallway,
wrapped in a dark blue towel. "Were you able to find
something for me to wear?"

Nodding, I pointed to the bedroom. "On the bed."

She disappeared through the doorway, and I exhaled heavily before following. "I'm sorry—"

"Stop apologizing," she snapped, dropping her towel,
and pulled on the T-shirt, the bottom of it stopping at
mid-thigh. "It's over. Do I wish you would have told me
what was happening from the start?" She glared at me,

shaking out the jeans before her, and sized them against her body before putting them on. "Yeah, I do. But I get it... Orders are orders." Her face scrunched up as she looked down at the jeans again. "How did you know my size?... How did you *have* jeans my size?"

Scratching the side of my face, torn between feeling guilty and amused, I shrugged. "They're from high school... I was a late bloomer." She pursed her lips and nodded, accepting my story. "Fuck the orders. Fuck Gaston. I will be dealing with him. If you want to go and live your life, then, by all means, you're free to go."

Tucking the T-shirt into the jeans, Belle peered up at me through her damp hair. "I'm free to go? Just like that? What about my father? Is he free?"

With everything happening, I had completely forgotten about her father. I cursed under my breath, rubbing the back of my neck. "I'll... I'll figure it out, okay? Once I take care of Gaston, I'll call in some favors."

"Favors..." She sighed, searching the nearly bare bookshelf I had pushed against the wall. "You really are deep in the Cinder Crew, aren't you?"

"I've done my fair share of shitty things, that's for sure. But I'm over it. I'm done with that life... Belle, after losing you..." I swallowed thickly. "You were the best thing that ever happened to me," I admitted.

Glancing over her shoulder at me, her eyebrows knit together. "And you were going to sell me?"

"No." I stepped forward. "Gaston wanted me to torture you so you'd accept him when he 'saved' you." I made air quotation marks and rolled my eyes. "I wasn't going to let him do that. But with the cameras and him threatening to hurt someone else... I had to come up with a plan first. Chris made that all slightly easier."

Flopping down on my bed with a book in hand, she waved me away. "Go. Shower. We have all day to discuss this."

I stared at her, wondering if she would take my duffel bag and disappear while I showered. I kind of hoped she would. I deserved it. "There's money in the bag by the door," I said before turning on my heel and heading into the bathroom without waiting for her response.

Twisting the water on as hot as I could stand, I stood beneath the spray and let the heat soak into my bones. I scrubbed at least three times, trying to wash the filthy, horrible feeling from my soul. I was a horrible person. A murderer, rapist... The one person I cared for more than anything in this godforsaken disgusting world, I imprisoned and let starve for three days. *Three*. I abused her. I didn't deserve her.

I shut the water off and watched the soapy water circle the drain before stepping out and wrapping myself with a towel. Wiping the mirror with my hand, I assessed the situation on my face. A short beard was growing that didn't look too awful. I brushed my teeth, grabbed a razor, and brought both out with me to pack.

Bracing myself for the empty bedroom, I slowed my pace and poked my head in the doorway. Belle was curled up with a book from my shelf, fast asleep in the center of my bed. My heart slammed against my ribs, simultaneously breaking and happy she didn't leave... because she should have...

Letting her sleep, I got dressed and took our soiled clothes to the dumpster.

Sixteen

Belle

THE FRONT DOOR SHUTTING woke me with a start. Disoriented, I stumbled from the bed, trying to find a place to hide. Strong arms wrapped around me before I could fall on my face, pulling me against a solid chest. Adam's familiar scent hit me, earthy and smokey like coffee.

"Easy, little rabbit, it's just me," his voice rasped through the turmoil in my mind. "You're safe."

I'm safe. The words cut through me, and tears began uncontrollably spilling down my face, soaking into his dark shirt. *I'm safe. What does fucking* safe *mean anymore?*

He held me tight, rubbing my back in soothing circles as I let go of all the emotions I'd been drowning in for the past week. I wasn't the hero from my books; I was the damsel in distress, and I was furious.

"I'm weak and pathetic," I sobbed, pulling away from him, and shoved my palms against my eyes, trying to halt the flow of tears. "Look at me! I'm useless!"

His hands gripped my forearms, pulling my hands from my face and forcing me to look at him. "I'm looking at you," he said, running a finger under my chin and tipping my head back. "You're not useless, weak, *or* pathetic."

Avoiding his eyes, I mumbled, "I couldn't save Ella or myself..."

"You saved *me*."

I glanced back at him, waiting for the punchline, but the sincerity in his face caught me off guard. My bottom lip trembled. "How?"

"You're the reason I'm getting out of Cinder Crew. I don't want to be a cold-blooded killer... I'm tired of the torture and living on the line, constantly looking over my shoulder. I want quiet. I want to do the things you want to do... I want you, Belle. I want to live my life with you."

Tracing the shadow wolf on his bicep, I shook my head. "I'm no one, Adam..."

He kissed me gently and innocently, another surprise. "You are to me. You don't need to make any decisions right now, but we need to leave. Gaston is probably on his way now looking for you."

"I need to tell you." I licked my lips, goosebumps breaking across my arms. "Our breakup... Gaston knew we were together and threatened to kill you if I didn't leave. He said he'd give you an impossible mission..."

"You were protecting me?" He chuckled wryly, his jaw tensing. "That fucker. What a fucking mess..."

My stomach tightened with anxiety. "Where are we going to go?"

Tucking stray hairs in my face behind my ear, he smiled. "Got a place on the water ready for us." He took my hand and kissed my knuckles. "First, I need to get you somewhere safe so I can meet with Gaston."

"I want to go with you." I straightened myself up, pushing away the nagging feelings of worry and fear. "I want to be the one to confront him. I want to be the one to put the knife in his heart."

Adam grinned, pride shining in his eyes. "Alright, little rabbit. If you insist."

For some reason, I thought it wouldn't take long to find Gaston. Adam would drive to his place, and we'd walk in, and that would be that. But... it wasn't like in my books. We had to search and find leads to where the man was hiding. He had gotten word that Priscilla was dead and immediately ran with his tail between his legs. Adam even raided his office, discovered several hard drives with his name on them, and destroyed them.

Some brave man, I thought in annoyance, following Adam back into his apartment. After hours of nothing new, we hit up a Walmart and got me some new shoes, clothes, and steaks for dinner. Setting my bags on the table, I dug through the fast-food bag and shoved three fries into my mouth.

Adam handed me my strawberry shake before heading into the kitchen to put away the groceries. After three days without food, I deserved a reward. Apparently, Adam felt the same way, having picked out the best cuts of steak he could find at a Walmart.

"Now what? If he's in hiding, does that mean we're safe and don't need to go to the safe house?" I asked, taking my bag of fries to the couch, and flopped down.

"We should, but I think a night here will be fine." Adam walked out of the kitchen with a plastic bag full of other bags and dropped them on the table. He made his way to me and knelt between my legs, kissing my thigh.

I giggled, setting my food beside me, and reached for his face. "I—"

"Beast!" Gaston's voice roared through the door as he pounded on it. "I know you're in there! Open up!"

Adam leaped to his feet, his muscles tightening as he stood protectively before me, glaring at the front door. "I knew it was too fucking quiet." He growled, his jaw clenching as Gaston slammed his fist against the door again. The wood cracked as he kicked it.

"I know you have her, Beast!"

Moving to open the door, Adam twisted and tackled me to the ground as gunfire popped off in the hallway. The door exploded in splinters, and the doorknob clattered to the ground.

Crouching in front of me, Adam growled over his shoulder, "Hide in the bedroom." I scrambled to the room, shutting and locking the door.

Frantically, I searched the room for a weapon, hoping I'd find a gun to press against Gaston's head and—

In the living room, I could hear Gaston enter and laugh menacingly. "Where is she, Beast?"

"She's gone, Gaston. She doesn't want you, so leave her alone."

I threw open his nightstand, finding condoms, an empty pack of cigarettes, and some random papers. Frowning, I looked behind the nightstand and under the mattress, turning up with nothing. I went to the closet, and the sounds of a physical altercation crashed through the wall.

Nothing... Nothing... Nothing... I growled in frustration pulling out a heavy box that had photos in it, and climbed on top to look on the shelf. A hunting knife greeted me. I grabbed it, shoved it in my waistband, and covered it with my shirt. Rushing to the door, I opened it as the gun went off.

I froze, my heart lodged in my throat. I couldn't even swallow.

Gaston laughed crazily. "What happened, Beast? Did you

have a change of heart? Too kind and gentle now to even defend yourself?"

"Stop!" I shouted, hurrying into the room. Adam looked up at me from the floor, clutching his arm, blood seeping between his fingers. "Gaston, what are you doing here?" I demanded, sidestepping broken glass on the floor.

Swiping his hair from his face, Gaston turned to me. "Belle! My dear! I'm here to save you from this monster." He glared at Adam. "I heard all of the horrible things he's done to you! Including having your poor old dear father locked up. But rest assured, my love, you're safe now! Your father has even been released and is waiting for you at your home because of me." He smiled smugly, waiting expectantly for me to rush to him and thank him.

"You're crazy," I muttered, wrapping my arms around my stomach, resting my hand on the knife snug against my hip.

Gaston blinked in genuine surprise. "Excuse me?" he stammered, the façade dropping from his face. "You insufferable ungrateful *bitch*. I'm saving your life, and *this* is how you're thanking me? Calling *me* CRAZY!" He stomped his boot-clad foot, the sound reverberating across the room with a thud.

"Save me? I don't need saving!" I snarled.

Another wave of shock crossed his face. "Whatever do you mean? Did this monster not kidnap you and leave you to starve for three days!?"

Glancing from Adam to Gaston, I narrowed my eyes at him. "And dear, Gaston, *how* would you have known that?"

Gaston stuttered, the wheels working overtime to form an excuse. "I was told."

"You had him kidnap me. *You* had him torture me. All to sweep in and try to be the hero. Even if this were not orchestrated, I would never fall for the likes of *you*." I sneered, stepping closer to him.

Flabbergasted, Gaston's face darkened to a crimson red, and a wide range of expressions flickered across it before settling on rage. "You... *whore!*" he shouted, looking ready to have a full-blown tantrum. He shook the gun at the ground, seething. "All the things I did for *you!* This is... unacceptable! I'll have *both* your skulls made into matching lamps for my mantel!"

Adam lunged at him, pinning his arms to his sides in a bear hug. Gaston dropped the gun, trying to shake free of Adam's hold. "How dare you!" he shrieked.

Unsheathing the knife in my waistband, I sank it deep

into Gaston's neck. His eyes widened dramatically, and his mouth fell open in a silent scream. I jerked the blade out, barely avoiding the spray of blood that was unleashed with the motion. He glared at me, baring his teeth as if to curse me.

As he quickly began fading, a surge of rage overcame me...

This is the man who harassed me for years! This is the man who took happiness from me! This is the man who had me locked in a cell and tortured! This fucking man! After every thought, I stabbed him in the face. His look of anger was replaced with pain and horror until nothing was left of it. I sunk the blade into his eye and twisted it straight to the hilt, then yanked it out, pulling his eyeball free from the socket.

Gaston slumped in Adam's arms, his face a mess of torn flesh and muscle. Adam dropped him to the floor and shook his good arm out, blood dripping from his fingertips. He looked down at himself and sighed. "I need to shower."

"What about your arm! Did he shoot you?" I dropped the knife and grabbed Adam's arm, peeling the sleeve away from his wound. "You need to get to a hospital!" I gasped, looking for something to stop the bleeding.

Adam chuckled, wiping his hand off on his pant leg. "You

just massacred Gaston's face, and you want to take me to the hospital? No hospitals. It only grazed me anyway… I need to clean up." He looked at me with a grin. "*You* need to clean up. Then you can suture it for me. I have supplies in the bathroom."

Seventeen

Adam

BELLE DIDN'T LEAVE MY side all through my shower. Literally. She helped me undress, then stripped and climbed in with me. She washed herself first, then turned to me, scrubbing the blood from my body.

Grabbing herself a towel, she stepped out. "I'll be right back," she said, disappearing from the room. I groaned, disappointed the shower didn't turn into more. My arm throbbed at the thought, and I scowled at it.

Pride didn't cover the feeling I had for Belle and how she took down Gaston. All the pent-up anger had spilled out of her tiny body straight into his face. It was a fitting way for him to die. Mutilated. The one thing he cared about more than anything else literally ripped away from him. It was glorious. I wanted to fuck her on the coffee table with his corps watching... If I hadn't been injured and covered in Gaston's blood, I would have.

Okay, that's weird. I cringed at myself and shut off the water, taking the towel Belle offered me. She was dressed in the clothes we just bought her: a screen-printed T-shirt with blue flowers and a pair of blue jeans that fit her much better than mine did. She placed a hand towel over my wound, and I held it in place as I made my way to the bedroom and sat on the bed. She already had the supplies out and ready on the nightstand.

"You set this up quick... I didn't even see you grab it from the bathroom," I commented, allowing her to move my hand and access the damage on my right arm.

"You're lucky I even *let* you shower," she retorted. "At least the bleeding has slowed... but you've lost a lot. Let me take you to the hospital."

I shook my head. "Not in this town. I'll go when we get to the safe house."

She eyed me for a moment, then nodded, cleaning the area with rubbing alcohol. I groaned, gritting my teeth as my arm burned in pain. "Fuck!"

"You're choosing this!" she snapped. "You could have gone to the hospital and been numbed, but you're stubborn. Now, hold still." She carefully threaded a needle and skillfully began suturing up the wound. "You're lucky the bullet didn't lodge in your arm," she whispered.

I watched her in silent awe, trying my best not to flinch as she worked. She tied off the thread and clipped it with scissors, running another clean cotton ball full of rubbing alcohol over it. I winced, biting my tongue to keep from shouting in pain.

"There," she announced. "All set. Let me wrap it for you." She picked up some gauze and a roll of bandages from the nightstand.

"Thank you," I mumbled, letting her bandage me up.

She leaned back, admiring her work. "If it weren't for you, I wouldn't have been able to..." she trailed off, her eyes lowering to her hands. "What are we going to do now?"

I took her hand. "We're going to go to the safe house. I'll have my men take care of things here. But until then..." I pulled her to me, wrapping my good arm around her, and kissed her. She eagerly returned the kiss, straddling my lap.

She ran her hands up my chest, stopping on my shoulders. "Will we be safe here?"

"Safe…" I grinned, tucking a stray hair behind her ear. "Baby, I've seen what you can do with a knife," I growled, leaning forward pressing my lips to hers. "I think we're beyond worrying about that now." I kissed down her chin to her neck, stopping at the tender flesh under her earlobe. I grazed my teeth against the skin there, earning a satisfying gasp that made my cock twitch. I rolled her onto her back, threw my towel, and straddled her. We stared at each other for a moment, searching each other's eyes.

"I missed this," she whispered, running her fingers over my tattoo. "I've missed being with you."

I kissed her. "I missed you too."

She cupped my face gently. "I'm sorry I left." She bit her bottom lip, dragging her fingers down my chest.

"You didn't have a choice." I kissed her. "And if you hadn't, I would have never changed," I murmured against her lips, coaxing her tongue into my mouth. She stroked her tongue against mine, pulled it into her mouth, and sucked on it before releasing me. I leaned my forehead against hers. "After all I put you through this week… Is this what you want?"

"Yes." She kissed me, humming as I passionately kissed her back. She wrapped her fingers around my cock, pulling me closer to her. "I want *you*."

Growling softly, I bit at her neck and sucked hard, marking her. "I need you," I whispered huskily, helping her remove her shirt and toss it to the floor. I let my eyes wander over her perfect breasts, nipples pert and hard with arousal. I groped her left breast and massaged it gently. I lowered my mouth to her other nipple, taking it between my teeth. She moaned in pleasure, her body arching into me.

She stroked me, running her fingers over my tip, gasping when I ran my tongue around her nipple and sucked it again. I moved my free hand, undoing her pants. She let me go to help take them off, kicking them onto the floor. I dipped my fingers between her legs, finding her already wet.

I groaned as she ran her hand over the tip of my cock, then gripped my shaft and pumped. I rubbed a half circle around her clit, slipping a finger and then two inside her. She moved her hand faster, and I let go of her nipple and pressed my mouth against hers, flexing my fingers up and rubbing the sensitive spot behind her clit. She moaned in my mouth, breaking away panting.

She released my cock as I kissed my way down her stomach and between her legs. "Adam," she whimpered as my tongue replaced my fingers. She grabbed my head, gripping my hair as her hips lifted from the bed.

I thrust my tongue into her, earning another gasp. Her thighs tightened around my head, encouraging me deeper into her. Lightening raced through my body straight to my cock at the sweet taste of her. I swirled my tongue around the bundle of nerves, dipping inside her core. I pulled her left leg up on my shoulder, opening her further for easier access. Her head leaned back against the bed as she cried out my name, a delicious moan following.

"Come for me, little rabbit," I growled, adding more pressure against her clit as she rocked into me. Her body tensed, shattering as she climaxed in my mouth. Her pussy pulsated around my tongue as I ate her out.

I lowered her leg, playing with her as she came down from her orgasm. "I want to feel you in me," she whimpered.

After another stroke, I knelt between her legs and kissed her, letting her taste herself on me. She reached greedily for my cock, guiding me to her pussy. "Now," she panted, rubbing me against her clit before sliding me to her opening. "I need you."

My breath caught as I pushed into her, filling her with thrust after thrust. The warm tightness of her body was like ecstasy around my shaft. She moaned into my shoulder, her fingernails digging into my back.

"You feel so good," she panted, grinding into me, matching my pace. "I want to ride you... I want to make you come."

I moaned, shoving myself into her again before pulling out and letting her climb on top of me. She kissed me, biting my lower lip gently as she lowered herself onto me. I grasped her hips as she gyrated on me, riding me hard.

"Fuck, Belle," I rumbled in her ear, feeling her body tighten around me. She breathed in sharply, clinging to me as she reached her climax, crying out my name. Her pussy bounced on my cock as it squeezed me. I growled, thrusting deeply into her, and released, holding her tightly against me.

Eighteen

Belle

DESIRE COURSED THROUGH ME, my body aflame like a live electric wire. Adam held me with his good arm, our breathing matched as we came down from our climax. I sat up, observing his near godlike body, his cock still buried deep within me.

"It's too bad we have to leave..." I sighed, running a finger down the center of his chest.

His hips lifted, and I moaned at the pressure against my cervix. "I could do a round two," he whispered huskily, helping me move on him again.

I moaned, my toes curling. "I want to, but..." His thumb grazed against my clit, and I jolted. "Ah! Stop, it's..." My body shuddered "...too sensitive."

He moved his hand away and chuckled. "Sorry, darlin'." He slowed his pace as I regained my composure.

"I want to keep going... But I need a minute. And we really should leave." With the body in the next room and neighbors not only next door but below... The paranoia of the police being called was beginning to get to me.

Adam ran his fingers up my thigh. "You're right. We should head out."

"What happens to Cinder Crew now that Gaston's dead?" I whispered, untangling from him to clean up.

He followed me to the bathroom. "I'll take over," he grunted, running a damp washcloth over himself.

"You're going to run it then?" I asked, sitting on the toilet, waiting for him to move from the sink.

He wandered off to the bedroom. "Probably not. It's a lot of work." His voice carried to me, followed by the sounds of clothes rustling.

I washed my hands and met him in the bedroom. He had on a new pair of jeans and a dark grey T-shirt, his dirty clothes in a pile next to his feet. "I want to travel the world," I said, putting on my pants and T-shirt, the ones he had given me earlier. "It's a dream of mine."

Scooping up his clothes, he carried them to the living room, where Gaston's body had already begun to smell. "Where would you like to go?"

I crinkled my nose, trying my best to ignore Gaston. Shoving his clothes into one of the grocery bags from earlier, Adam set them on the table and put his hands on his hips.

"Japan would be fun," I said softly, taking my new socks and shoes from one of the bags on the table. "Or Italy."

He smiled. "That can be arranged," he said, going to the fridge with two empty bags, filling one with ice and the other with the groceries we recently bought. "We better let the clean-up crew come in before this gets too bad."

My eyes darted from Gaston back to Adam. "Do you think he was telling the truth about my father being free?"

Packing everything together, Adam smiled reassuringly at me. "I'll make sure of it," he said, planting a kiss on the side of my head as he passed me to the door. "Come on, little rabbit, let's get out of here."

I fell asleep on the ride to the safehouse, Adam's hand resting on my thigh the entire way. After he let me kill Gaston, a new feeling surged through me for him. I wasn't a damsel in distress, and I proved it by sinking that blade into Gaston's jugular.

"We're here." He patted my leg, waking me from my twilight sleep.

Rubbing my eyes, I glanced at the large house lit up like a Christmas tree against the night sky. Opening the car door, the smell of the ocean hit me with a gentle breeze. In the distance, I could hear the waves crashing and birds squawking.

Adam came to my side and wrapped his arm around my shoulders. "Home for a few months... Until I can secure us something better." He pressed his lips to my temple.

"It's beautiful." I leaned into his embrace, enjoying the

moment between us but also excited to explore.

Taking our belongings from the trunk, Adam shot me a mischievous grin. "There's a surprise inside for you." He tipped his head to the front door.

"For me?" My eyebrows knit together in confusion.

He nodded, carrying as much as he could with his injured arm toward the house. "Come on." As the words left his mouth, the front door swung open, revealing a beautiful woman with long blonde hair.

"Belle!" Ella called out, racing down the steps, her hair flying behind her like a cape.

I ran to her, the two of us colliding in a tight embrace and sinking to the ground. "Ella! Ella, you're here!" I half laughed, half cried. Memories of horrors we endured together hit and melted away like snow on a warm afternoon. Even the betrayal I felt toward her melted away when I saw how happy she looked. The experiences we shared bonded us, but they wouldn't define us.

"I can't believe it! Chris just told me when you pulled up. I'm so happy to see you!" She pressed her hands against my face, locking eyes with me. "We did it, babe, we survived."

I nodded, brushing tears from my face. "We did."

Helping me to my feet, Ella pulled me toward the house. "Let me give you the grand tour!" She giggled, looping her arm through mine. I glanced over my shoulder at Adam watching us in amusement.

He waved me off. "Go. Enjoy yourself. I'll make dinner," he said, following us inside. Chris met him in the foyer, the two exchanging greetings and hardy handshakes. "Help me bring the rest of this stuff in," Adam grunted, the two heading back out into the night.

Ella and I smiled at each other and hurried off into the house, Ella guiding me through the maze of rooms. We ended up outside on the back porch, watching the moon over the ocean. She held my hand, just like when we were in the cells. My thumb brushed over her knuckles as she leaned her head against my shoulder.

"Are you happy?" she asked, her eyes twinkling in the glow of the moon.

I sighed. "I will be. I'm still processing this week." I rolled my eyes up to the sky. "I killed Gaston. I thought I'd feel differently if I killed someone... Sad or scared. But I don't. I feel... liberated."

Ella squeezed my hand. "I understand. I killed a few people... including Priscilla. I don't feel bad at all. I feel the same, liberated."

"She had it coming," I blurted out. We looked at each other and grinned.

"She did," Ella giggled.

Adam walked out onto the porch, the smell of steak following him. "You ladies enjoying yourselves?" He stuck a cigarette between his lips and lit it.

"You're just hoping to catch some action between us," Ella joked.

Chris's voice cut through from the kitchen, "Not without me!"

She smirked, letting go of my hand, and sauntered into the kitchen.

Adam chuckled, sidling up next to me, blowing smoke into the air. "What do you think?"

"Kind of hoping you'll quit smoking so I can have a library one day," I said with a small smile.

He looked from me to the cigarette in his hand and snuffed it. "I should have known... Not like you worked at a library for no reason." He patted his pockets, pulling out a small black phone.

I raised an eyebrow at it as he held it out to me. "A phone?"

"Mhm. It's yours for now, until I can get you something more permanent. I picked it up when we stopped for gas. I just loaded it with minutes. I made some calls... Your father is home and doing well. You should call him."

Grabbing the phone, I flipped it open and dialed the number I had memorized since childhood. It rang twice before my father's familiar voice picked up. "Papa... It's me," I choked out. "I'm safe."

Adam patted me on the back before heading into the house. I leaned against the balcony with a sigh of relief, listening to my father sob on the other side. "I had to leave for a little bit. But I'll be home again soon. Gaston is dead, Papa. He won't bother us anymore."

Epilogue

Adam, Five Years Later

Somewhere in a secluded spot in Alabama.

IT WAS LATE IN the afternoon, the summer heat still in full effect but the cool breeze off the ocean made it bearable. Chris stretched out beside me in the sand, the pale grains a stark contrast against his reddening skin. I chuckled softly, the sound barely breaking above the crash of the waves. It was perfect, paradise out here.

I brushed the sand from my legs outstretched before me, catching a glimpse of the gunshot wound on my bicep from Gaston. It had healed nicely, thanks to Belle, but the reminder was a gut punch nearly every time I looked at it. A reminder of when I almost lost myself...

"Can you believe this shit?" Chris said, squinting at the horizon where the sea met the sky in an endless kiss. "From blood-stained streets to sipping coconut water with our toes in the sand.'

"Never thought we'd make it, did ya?" I flicked a glance at him, the perpetual tension having eased from his shoulders as he watched the girls playing at the edge of the ocean. I turned my attention to them, Belle's laughter carrying over the water, pure and unguarded. She chased Ella, her hair whipping behind her like a banner. Ella's shrieks of delight cut through the air. They danced at the water's edge, dodging the foamy residue as they splashed each other.

Warmth spread across my chest as I watched Belle dance with reckless abandon, genuine happiness creasing her eyes. Comfort looked good on her. She had filled out a bit, her hips and thighs curvier. The sun had given her skin a golden glow and even bleached her hair a bit. "Look at 'em, Chris. They're somethin' else."

"Like fucking phoenixes rising from the ashes," Chris said in awe, watching as Ella threw her head back, the sun turning her blonde hair into a halo of fire. Her skin had tanned, and like Belle, she had become relaxed.

"Remember when they first came into our world? How broken everything seemed?" I shook the memories from my head. "Now, just look." The two were attached at the hip, having become close like sisters. They did nearly everything together, even insisting we build houses next to each other.

"Times change, people change," Chris grunted.

I glanced at him, noticing the way he was staring at his hands as though he could still see the blood on them. He shoved them in the sand, turning his attention back to the girls, his face sobering.

"Never thought I'd see you go soft, Chris," I teased, nudging him with my elbow.

"Soft?" he barked out a laugh. "Just adapting to thrive, brother. Nothing soft about that."

I nodded and mulled over what he said. "Surviving's one thing," I mused. "But living—really living with these women—that's something else."

"Damn right." He watched as Ella spun, arms wide, embracing the freedom we never knew was possible. Belle caught her, and together, they collapsed onto the sand in a fit of laughter. "Let's keep it that way," he said, his tone dropping.

"We will," I promised, a vow forged in the fires of hell we'd walked through to keep those two women safe.

We'd lived by the code, but now, the only code we had was keeping our lives safe. Happy. The island was our sanctuary, a place where the darkness of our past couldn't reach us, couldn't touch the women who'd become our redemption. Belle even encouraged me to reach out to my family and fix the ties that had been severed by Gaston and Priscilla. It took me two years to work up the courage, and I was shocked when I was welcomed back with open arms.

"Come on, let's rustle up some grub for the ladies," he stood, brushing sand from his shorts. "Bet they're starving after all that frolicking."

I chuckled. "Lead the way, Chef Charming," I quipped, getting to my feet.

"Fuck off," Chris shot back with a smirk. There was no longer any bite to his words. As much as he hated to admit, Ella had changed him as well. Broke through that wall and rebuilt the man before me.

We strode across the sand, two men who had walked through fire and come out the other side, not unscathed, but alive. Alive and fucking determined to never slip back into the darkness that once claimed us. This island, this peace—it was ours, and we'd be damned if anything threatened it.

The sun dipped low, setting the sky ablaze in shades of

orange and crimson. A breeze carried the scent of salt and charred meat as Chris and I manned the grill like a couple of domesticated warlords, turning our blades into spatulas.

I glanced up at Chris, wondering if he was thinking the same thing as I was. "Shit, man, remember when our biggest worry was whether the feds had us on wiretap?" I flipped a burger, the sizzle cutting through the quiet hum of the waves.

"Fuck that noise," he grunted, spearing a slab of steak, the juice running down his wrist. "This is the life. No more looking over our shoulders."

"Damn straight." I clinked my beer bottle against his. We shared a nod, a silent oath to the lives we'd clawed out of the dirt.

"Food's about ready," Chris called over to the beach where Belle and Ella were soaking up the last of the day's rays.

Belle rose, brushing sand from her swimsuit and helping Ella to her feet. Her eyes lifted to me, a slow smile crossing her face. It took my breath away for a moment. I knew I loved her from the moment I met her, but every day, I had a new reason why.

Belle

GRAINS OF SAND CLUNG to my feet and legs, the remnants of a perfect day on the beach. Looping my arm through Adam's, we followed behind Ella and Chris, listening to their playful banter to the small dining area. The men had set up folding chairs and created a table with two coolers and a towel.

"Never thought I'd say this, but your cooking might just be better than your right hook," Ella teased him, her eyes sparkling as his face lit up with amusement.

"Only thing I do better is love you," he shot back, his voice carrying a softness to it that had grown over the past few years.

"Ah, you two are giving me diabetes with all this sweetness," I quipped with a giggle, enjoying their pretend argument.

"Sit down, babe, let the men work." Chris winked at Ella. To complete the homemaker look, all he needed was an apron that said, 'Kiss the cook.'

We gathered around the table. An ensemble of survivors feasting, not just on grilled delights, but on the second chance we'd snatched from fate's clutches.

I caught Adam's eye as I lifted a drink to him. He clinked his beer with mine and winked, the action causing a fluttering inside my stomach. "To my night in shining armor," I whispered to him.

He rumbled with laughter, pressing a kiss to my temple. "To the savior of my soul, my queen."

The moon was rising as we said our goodbyes. The gentle ocean breeze felt good against sun-kissed skin as we trudged to our home, nearly next door to Ella and Chris's. It was paradise; everything about it was perfect.

Adam followed me into the living room, his arms snaking around my waist. He dropped his chin on my shoulder. "I love you," he murmured in my ear.

I twisted in his arms, kissing his lips. "I love you," I whispered, leaning my forehead against his.

"I have a surprise for you."

Sitting back on my heels, I looked up at him curiously. "What kind of surprise?"

"Come with me." He took me by the hand and led me to the office. I stalled in confusion, looking from the closed door to him. "Inside the office?"

He grinned, a genuinely excited expression that lit up every inch of his face. "Close your eyes. It's a surprise."

Obliging, I closed my eyes and waited. The door opened, and he took my hands, leading me into the room. "Can I open them?"

"No, no... Hang on." He let go of my hands and turned on the lights. I giggled, wondering what in the world could be in the office that would surprise me.

"Okay... Now you can."

I opened my eyes and gasped. While we spent the day at the beach, he had converted the office into a library. I spun around, looking at the wall-to-wall bookcases filled with books, a small reading nook area in front of the window, and comfortable chairs where the desk had been.

"Adam... How did you do this all in one day?"

He chuckled, catching me as I threw myself at him and hugged him. "I hired some people. They started as soon as we left. Do you like it?"

"Like it? I love it!" I kissed him, breaking away to look around once more. "I can't believe it... You even have my favorite books!" I pulled a large fantasy book from the shelf.

He leaned against the door frame. "Anything to make you happy, little rabbit."

Putting the book back, I went to him and pulled him into the room. "I love you," I whispered, kissing him. "*You* make me happy."

With a growl, he lifted me up and carried me from the library. "Oh yeah? Let me show you how happy you make me." He nuzzled my neck.

I squealed in laughter as he took me into the bedroom and dropped me on the bed. "Wasn't that what the library was for?" I bit my lip, watching him strip his shirt off, desire flooding through me.

He smirked, crawling onto the bed between my legs. "Can't I show you too?" He pulled down my skirt and swimsuit bottoms.

I kicked them off onto the floor and removed my top. "Always." I giggled, tossing my top across the room.

Sitting back, he licked his lips as he looked me over, running his hands up my thighs. "Roll over."

I flipped over onto my stomach, and he straddled me, his hands running over my back. "You're gorgeous," he whispered, brushing his lips against my spine. "I'm a lucky son of a bitch." He rubbed my back, finding a knot, and worked on it carefully.

"I'm the one getting the back rub and got a new library! I'm the lucky one." I laughed, closing my eyes to enjoy his fingers running across my shoulders.

He kissed my shoulder blade. "Guess we're both lucky." He worked from my shoulders, down to my feet, massaging me until I was loose with relaxation.

Rolling me over onto my back, he continued massaging my

chest and breasts, taking his time with the more sensitive area. I moaned as he slipped a finger inside me, then two. He kissed my thigh as he stroked me. Once I was panting and lifting my hips, he pulled himself from his shorts and rubbed the tip of his cock against my entrance.

He pressed inside me with a soft grunt, slowly filling me to the core. I moaned as he pulled back and thrust into me again. Gradually, his pace increased, his teeth grazing my collarbone. I matched his rhythm, dragging my nails down his back, begging him to go harder.

"Don't hold back. I want all of you. Fuck me hard, Adam." I snaked my hand between my legs, rubbing my clit as his movement became erratic, his hands gripping my hips. My body began to tense, and I screamed his name as I came, my pussy gripping his cock, drawing him into me.

"Fuck, Belle," he moaned, slamming into me as his own orgasm exploded from him. He bucked his hips with a grunt, brushing his lips against mine. "Ah... Damn, I could do this all night." He sighed, rolling off me.

I smiled, climbing on top of him before he could get up. "Then let's do it."

His hands rested on my thighs, the corner of his mouth turning up in a smirk. "As you wish, my queen."

Lowering myself on top of him, I kissed him passionately, the ending to my favorite fairy tale playing through my head, *and they lived happily ever after...*

About the Author

MK RICHBERGER IS A multi-genre author who enjoys listening to loud music, especially emo.

She met her house spouse fishing for cans and guppies. Together, they enjoy their life with their two kids, two cats, and a timid dog.

Also by MK Richberger

MK Richberger

Fantasy

Between The Worlds

Journey

Morning Star

MYSTERY

The Kingston Trial

ROMANCE

Northern Lights

Beastly Savage

Riding Savage

MFK R
Horror/Thriller

Scout: Bound With Blood

Feral

Earthworm and Other Twisted Stories

Made in the USA
Las Vegas, NV
01 July 2024

91763055R00095